William Osborn Stoddard

Tom and the money king

William Osborn Stoddard

Tom and the money king

ISBN/EAN: 9783744737241

Printed in Europe, USA, Canada, Australia, Japan

Cover: Foto ©Andreas Hilbeck / pixelio.de

More available books at **www.hansebooks.com**

Tom and the Money King

BY

WILLIAM O. STODDARD

ILLUSTRATED BY

CHARLES EDWARD BOUTWOOD

ST. PAUL
THE PRICE-MCGILL COMPANY
455–473 CEDAR STREET

PRINTED AND PLATED BY
THE PRICE-McGILL COMPANY
ST. PAUL, MINN.

CONTENTS.

ILLUSTRATIONS.

TOM AND THE MONEY KING.

CHAPTER I.

AWAY UP IN THE WORLD.

It was a gas-lighted passageway on the lower floor of a vast building, and several men and women who had business on the upper floors were stepping quickly along to reach the elevator, the door of which was open at the end of the passage. The moment that the last of them squeezed in, the door was pushed shut by a boy who sat upon a stool inside with his hand upon the starting-line of the elevator. As he closed the door, he pulled the line, and the heavily loaded box began to move upward. He was a dark-haired, wiry-looking boy, of apparently about fifteen years, and the expression of intense watchfulness in his bright, black eyes seemed to belong to them. His dress was neat, but plain, and he had the responsible air of a pilot steering a big ship.

The first man to enter that elevator, when it was empty, had stepped right across it to its one bench and sat down, and he was completely hidden now, for all the rest were packed in front of him. He was of middle height, thin, but not slender, brown haired, nervous looking, and he had a noticeable cast in one of his flashing gray eyes. He carried in each hand an elegant black morocco case, not over a foot long and six or eight inches square. One of these he put down on the floor at his feet, and the other he held in his lap. He seemed to have forgotten them and all other things after he had said "Seventh floor" to the boy.

As for the boy, there he sat, perched upon his high stool, stopping and starting the elevator, opening and shutting its door, as passenger after passenger escaped from the box which carried him or her upstairs. He only gave the number of each floor as he reached it, but he spoke out sharply, and now he said "Seventh."

"Seventh!" echoed the man with the cast in his eye, and he shot out of the elevator as if he had been suddenly waked up and feared it might run away with him.

There was one more stoppage, letting out the last passenger, and then a start and another stop and the boy himself got down from his stool and stepped out.

"Ninth floor," he said to himself. "Top of the Probus building. One of those men that got out on the eighth-floor was the architect that built it. It's a big thing for a man to know enough to put up a building like this. They make loads o' money, too. I wish I knew more. I've got to if I'm going to rise in the world. I know enough to run an elevator now. That isn't much. Tell you what, though, I'm going up somehow!"

He wore a very resolute look as he said that, but his duty called him back into the elevator and down it went. It was stopped at the seventh floor, and two men who got in seemed excited.

"If Angus should die," remarked one of them, "the effect on the money market now would be something like an earthquake."

"He won't," replied the other man. "Dr. Harbeck says he'll be all right to-morrow."

"We must keep it a dead secret, anyhow," said the first speaker, and in a minute more the elevator was down and they were out.

The boy heard although he did not seem to, and he repeated the names to himself: "Dr. Harbeck, Angus, that's the money king, I know."

On the opposite side of the vast Probus building and near its main entrance, there was a row of four other elevators, and one of these a little later, on its way down, took in three gentlemen at the seventh floor. One of them was brown-haired with a cast in his left eye.

"My other case!" he suddenly exclaimed, as the elevator went down.

"You had but one when you came," said his nearest companion. "Did you start from home with two?"

"Where could I have left it?" came back, in a tone of intense annoyance.

"Oh, you'll get it back, Dr. Harbeck," said the third gentleman, confidently.

"Advertise for it. I'm glad it's no worse than you say for Mr. Angus."

"He must be careful"— and there the doctor checked himself, as if he feared to say too much, but his gray eyes were looking around anxiously, as if they were hunting for something. They seemed to pierce right into everything they looked at, and then they appeared to draw back as if they were searching his memory for the lost case or for the place where he had left it. He was evidently more than a little perplexed and disturbed. Neither of the three said anything more, and they separated when they left the elevator.

The machine managed by the boy on the other side of the building continued to go up and down in its noiseless way until nearly the close of business hours. At a little before five o'clock, it was nearing the third floor on one of its down trips, half full.

"Down!" shouted a shrill voice, and, as it stopped and the door flew open, in darted a short, thickset, red-headed boy, with a tin dinner-pail in his hand.

"Hello, Tom," he said. "You've got the elevator, have you? You'll break somebody's neck, first you know."

"I guess not," said Tom, quietly.

"Are you going to run it all vacation?"

"No, Gap, don't talk; you made me pass that man," exclaimed Tom.

"Hear him grumble at you," said Gap, but they reached the bottom in a second more, and while the rest got out Gap lingered to say:

"'Tisn't anything much to run an elevator. I could do it. Nothing but just sit there and start and stop it. Let me try it, one trip."

"No, you won't," said Tom, as Gap put out his hand for the rope. "Don't you touch it. 'Gainst orders. Pat was off duty and I took it for to-day."

"It'd be fun," said Gap, "but if I were you I wouldn't use up all my vacation that way."

"I sha'n't," said Tom; "I'm out of school for good. I'm not going back —"

"Oh," said Gap. "You've quit, have you? Now you'll be looking 'round for a place."

Off he went, jostling two or three people in his hurry, and pulling a couple of peanuts out of one of his pockets.

"I'd rather sit there," he said to himself, "and 'tend elevator, than run 'round on errands in hot weather. I guess Tom Tracy 'll find out what work is before long, though."

Tom and his machine were now at the top of the Probus building, and there seemed to be no need for haste in starting down again. He sat still on the stool and glanced around the empty elevator. There was plenty of glaring sunshine on that floor.

"Hello!" he exclaimed. "What's that."

He made a quick dash and pulled out something from under the bench.

"It isn't a banker's case," he said, as he turned it over and felt of its rich-looking morocco leather. "It isn't a lady's satchel. None of those boys carry such a thing. Who could ha' left it?"

He sat on the stool again and tried to recall the faces of his passengers. It was like a long procession going by in his memory, and he kept nodding his head and saying: "No—no—no—not his—not hers—not him," until he jumped up, exclaiming: "There! That's the man! I've got him! Had a twist is his eye. He carried two of them and he left this. There's no name on it, but the key's in it. I've got to find out who he was, but I'll have to wait till after we close up. I must put it away, now—"

He sprang like a flash, to a door near by with a key in it. Open flew the door, disclosing an empty room. Down went the case in the corner, there was a bang, a turn of a key in a lock, and Tom was back at his post, remarking: "It'll be safe there, anyhow."

Down went the elevator as if it had been sent for, and it had, indeed, more work to do, but the business day of all that part of the great city of New York was drawing toward its close.

The banks had shut their doors at three o'clock, and would not pay out or take in any more money, although their clerks and book-keepers had much to do, afterward, behind the closed doors. It was just so with the private bankers' and brokers' offices which closed at four o'clock, and with the great public offices, such at the sub-treasury, and with hundreds of great and small business houses. Whether they made money or lost money, they were all counting up and getting ready to go home. That was what was doing also at one business concern out of doors. This concern stood on a street corner, in front of a large brick building, one square below the Probus building. A low table stood there, with a lower table on each side of it, and a very short legged stool behind it. On the stool sat a tall, dark complexioned woman with a high nose, high cheek bones, and with an expression upon her face that was very much like one of contempt for everybody that passed by. You could see gray streaks in her coal black hair, for her scoop-shovel bonnet had fallen back, while she was bending over her table and counting her cash, as all the other business concerns were doing. She had a pile of nickels and coppers to count, and some silver, but no bills or checks or gold coins.

"It's been a good day," she said. "Seven dollars and sixty-seven cents. I've got to get some more peanuts. I'll have to go down to the wharf, good and early, after cocoanuts. Oranges? I'm glad I've got rid of so many—bananas, too—they were beginning to spoil. The gum drops are drying up! It's awful hot weather! I wish I knew who stole the lozenges. Four oranges missing, too. Wharf rats and gutter snipes! Thieves! If they don't look out! Well, it's been a pretty good day."

2

No doubt but that it was a prosperous peanut stand, but it had its annoyances and losses, like other business concerns. It's owner finished her counting, and then her long arms moved rapidly around her. The tables were cleared in a twinkling, and when her stock in trade was stowed in some baskets, which she pulled out from under the table, there did not seem to be a quarter so much of it as when it was spread out for sale. The tables themselves were placed in safety down a basement stairway belonging to the corner building, and the peanut stand had disappeared. All its varied stock of fruits and other eatables was about to be carried off by the hands of one old woman. She was standing and looking down at them, and she drew a long, sighing breath as she stooped to pick them up, for she was old and tired, and it was a very warm day.

"Here! Hold on! What do you mean?" she exclaimed, reaching out after her largest basket, as it suddenly got up and began to walk off.

"Come along, Mrs. Cathcart," sang out a cheery, boyish voice. "You bring those two and I'll carry this one as far as I go."

"Tom Tracy!" she said, with a swift change in her face. "Well, I declare! You're

"COME ALONG, MRS. CATHCART."

a good fellow. I'm an old woman, Tom. It's a hot day."

"I know it," said Tom. "I've got to hurry, too. I'll give you a lift, though. Got an errand down town."

She had picked up her two other baskets and was walking along with him. She walked slowly and with something very like dignity in her manner. Tom himself was willing not to go very fast, with that basket on his arm, and he remarked that he had been cooped up all day in an elevator, and had but just been set free. She asked about his elevator and things in the Probus building in a way that proved that she knew more than a little about her customers, old and young. She and Tom had walked only a couple of squares before they seemed to have walked out of one city and into another. There were not any magnificent buildings here, to right or left of them. Everything looked older, and Mrs. Cathcart turned out of the wide street along which they had walked, into a narrow, crooked thoroughfare, lined with dingy, rickety old structures, which looked, at that hour, as if nobody had any further use for them. It was a remnant of the very oldest part of the city, and it was fast passing away. Even the ground it stood on would soon be needed for new buildings of another sort. Right upon the corner, however, Tom stopped and put down his basket.

"I'm real sorry, Mrs. Cathcart," he said, "but I've got to go the other way. You haven't much farther to go."

"No, Tom, not far," she said, but with a very much gratified beam in her strongly lined old face, "Thank you very much. There are boys who wouldn't ha' dared to lug a basket for an old apple woman."

"I never thought o' that," said Tom, with a laugh. "Good-bye, Mrs. Cathcart."

Off he went, and she seemed to really feel better able to carry her whole load. She rested there for a moment, before she took it up. Everything in that side street ahead of her wore a deserted look. There were lines of carts and drays along the curbstones, but all the horses were gone. A few dingy little grocery shops were open, but nobody was going into or out of them. There was nothing in all that street to make any rattle, but nevertheless there were sounds of a curious kind coming out of an open window in the second story of a paintless, old, wooden shell, on the next corner beyond. There was a queer sort of corner grocery in the lower story of that building, and next to that an open door showed a badly kept flight of stairs. At the top of those stairs was a shut door, and the sounds came through that, as well as through the window.

Behind that door was one of the darkest rooms in all the world, and all its dark was locked in. The furniture of the room had a worn, old-fashioned look, and there was almost too much of it. Against the wall, on the side opposite the door, stood a very ancient looking piano, with ivory keys that were cracked and yellow with time, but the sounds that were coming from it proved that it was in good tune. White fingers, of a pair of small, well-shaped hands, were flitting along the keys, but their owner was not looking at them. She seemed, rather, to be letting them have their own way, for her eyes were shut, and her fair young face wore a dreamy look. It also had a look as if she were asking questions of somebody, and was troubled because no answer came.

"Stop! Stop! You're a lady! Peanuts! Peanuts! Great Crib!" suddenly screamed a loud, harsh voice, a little behind her.

That exclamation seemed to be replied to by another voice, in a long, full, trill, and the whole room rang with canary music from a cage that hung in the open window, where geraniums and other flowers and plants were prospering in the warm flood of summer sunshine.

Music, and light, and beauty, girl, and bird, and flowers, and yet that was a room which contained a great darkness.

"What a pipe! Great Crib!" screamed the first voice, and the white fingers ceased wandering over the piano.

The parrot, who sat upon a swinging bar, over a row of the flower boxes, was an uncommonly large and showy bird, and while he scolded the canary he twisted his head to bring one of his goggle eyes to bear upon the girl at the piano. Perhaps he thought that a young lady of fourteen or fifteen should not have let her glossy, brown hair, tumble down her shoulders so loosely. Her slight figure was now turned around upon the piano stool, and she was leaning toward the door, as if listening.

In the middle of the room was a square table, covered with a white cloth and arranged with cups, and saucers, and plates, as if supper were waiting for two, and a teakettle sat and sang upon a very small stove in one of the back corners. If the room had not been pretty large, there would have been too much in it, altogether, for several aged, well rubbed and battered trunks and chests sat lazily against the wall between its heavy old chairs. The young listener arose from the piano stool and walked around the table toward the door. As she passed the table, her hands hovered over it, like a pair of white birds, touching a plate here, a knife or fork there, the sugar bowl, the milk jug, the napkins, with a light, airy touch, that seemed to ask them if they all were in their places. One hand went out before her, as she went on toward the door, and when it reached the knob, it turned it, quickly. "Locked? Yes, locked," she said. "Of course. It must be locked. I ought not to want to get out, but I wish I could. It must be light somewhere."

The whole room was full of sunshine as she spoke, and at that moment a brighter gleam shot across her face.

"Coming! Coming! Lady! She's a lady!" screamed the parrot. "Peanuts! Great Crib! Hurrah!"

"Crib, Crib," said the girl, "do be still. She's late. Be quiet, Pete."

"Late! Late!" he shouted. "Coming! Lady! Bly! Bly! Bly!"

"Blind? Yes, Crib, Amy is blind," she said, as her feathered friends broke out into a queerly mingled chorus. "There, I can hear her."

No ears less acute than those of a bird or a blind person could have heard the slight sound at the foot of the stairs, but more was made as the feet of the lady peanut merchant came slowly up. In a moment more, a key was turned in the lock and in she walked, very warm and very weary.

"Amy, darling!" she said, as she opened her arms. "Grandmother!" said Amy, and then all the family that lived in that room were at home.

It was not quite six o'clock when Tom Tracy returned to the Probus building, from the errand which had enabled him to give old Mrs. Cathcart so good a lift homeward. The elevator was still running, with less frequent trips, but there was a small old man upon the stool instead of a boy. "Kedzie," said Tom, "will Pat be here to-morrow?"

"Your father said that he would, and that's all I know," replied a cracked, husky, crusty voice, out of one side of a wide, withered mouth. "Your father's up there now, and he asked if you'd got back. He's waiting for you."

That information was given with a shake of the head which plainly implied that it was an awful thing to be waited for by Tom's father, but Tom did not show any alarm, even if he felt any. He appeared to be in a hurry to go up, however, and Kedzie pulled the rope. There were no stops to make, and there was no time for impatience before the door was pushed open and Tom was out on the ninth floor.

"You'd better report at once," rasped Kedzie, and down he went, but his advice was not taken.

A key came out of Tom's pocket, the door of the empty room was opened, and the morocco case was in his hands.

"I hate to open it," he said, "but I've got to find out whose it is."

He waited for a breath or two, and then he added:

"It's just awful to turn a key that does n't belong to me. Hello!"

His fingers had done it for him, almost without asking his permission, in his eager excitement, and the inside of the case was before his eyes.

"I know what they are," he exclaimed. "They're doctor's tools. Cut a man all up. Lancits. Forceps. Don't know what that riggummagee is. Now, whom does it all belong to?"

The glittering litter of beautifully polished instruments lay upon a folded sheet of chamois leather, and as Tom lifted that he suddenly drew back his fingers as if he had touched something too hot, and uttered a loud startled, "Oh!"

Well he might, for there, at the bottom of the case, lay several packages of greenbacks, and a small, heavy, canvas bag.

CHAPTER II.

Tom Tracy stood still for a full half minute, staring down at the astonishing contents of that case. Then he stooped and lifted the packages of greenbacks and the bag, one after another, as carefully as if they had been so many sick people.

"Gold!" he said, as he put down the bag. "Hear it chink!"

His face was pale and his fingers had even trembled a little, but he was putting on a brave, determined look, as if he were not really much afraid of either the surgical instruments or the money. Nevertheless it did seem dangerous, somehow, to see it and to handle it, and that was precisely what he now felt compelled to do, searching carefully. It was of no use, however, for not a sign of a business-card, letter, address, nor anything else, written or printed, could he discover.

"It's dead sure to be advertised," he said,

28

"but I don't want to wait for that. I want to find the owner of it."

He stood in deep thought, for a minute or so, with his hands in his pockets. Then his face brightened.

"Hurrah!" he exclaimed. "I know. I heard them. Dr. Harbeck! Mr. Angus is sick in one of those seventh floor rooms, and they sent for him. I saw him. I'd know him again. Got a twist in his eye. I can find his name in the directory. I'm all right now."

He shut and locked the case, and put it down in a corner of the room, and heaped old newspapers over it. Then he walked out and locked the door behind him, and stood still in front of it.

"Of course," he said, "I'll speak to father about it. I wish he'd let me tell him just how it is, but he won't. Anyhow, I'll get some supper, and then I'll go after Dr. Harbeck."

He did not go to the elevator, on his way to supper, but through one of the passageways on that floor. In every direction but one there were corridors lined with business offices, but at the end of this there was a home, a family residence. Several very good, although not large rooms, on that upper floor, had been finished for people to live in, and had been set apart for the family of the janitor, the trusty and trusted keeper of that great business hive. He was a very important person, and not many people lived higher up in the world than he did, and Tom was his only son.

Mr. Tracy was the only man who knew all about the Probus building. Under his orders were all the other men and the boys and the scrub women who put its hundreds of rooms in order every evening, to be ready for the business men who were to enter them in the morning. Not only was he a very important man, but he knew that he was, and he looked exceedingly dignified, for a man of his size, as he stood by the supper table waiting for his wife to come in with the teapot. His son came in first, with a look of serious business on his face.

"Thomas," said Mr. Tracy, "I've heard no complaint of your management of the elevator. I felt that to put you there was a great risk. I'm glad nothing has happened. You may go out after supper. The door will be open for you at ten o'clock."

Every word came out as if he were a general in command, approving of the manner in which some gallant young officer had stormed a battery. He was rewarding the hero with a furlough, but instead of thanking him Tom broke out at once: "Father, I found something to-day. Left in the elevator. Great value—"

"Do you know the owner, Thomas?"

"I guess I do," said Tom. "I wanted to tell you about it. You ought to know what it is—"

"Stop, Thomas!" said his father, sharply. "If you know the owner, and can find him, I've no business to know any more. I won't know. Don't tell me. Don't tell anybody. If I should try to know too much in this building, it would ruin me. Mind that, Thomas. Never know too much. A boy that knows too much isn't worth a cent."

"I'll take it right to him," said Tom.

"That's all I want," said his father.

"And Tom doesn't want to be shut up in that elevator all vacation," added a very pleasant voice behind them.

A tall, portly lady was putting down a steaming teapot, and the rest of the table

talk was in her hands. Her view of the
the case was that the elevator was a kind
of summer prison for a boy just out of
school, while her husband regarded it as a
post of honor, a stepping-stone to higher
posts in the offices of business men. Tom
himself shared a little in both views, but
he did not have much to say, and finished
his supper rapidly. Shortly afterward, he
was out of the building and on his way up
town with a parcel, well wrapped up in
brown paper, under his arm. He had looked
into a directory; he knew where he was
going, and he was in a hurry. Even when
he reached the center of the world, in City
Hall square, he did not pause. The great
suspension bridge over the East River ends
there, close by the end of the elevated railway, and there is a tall, electric telegraph
post at the curbstone, and the center of the
world is believed to be at the foot of that
pole. Tom may not have known it. At all
events he darted up the stairway to the elevated railway station, and into a closely
packed train. Not a great while afterward he
was standing in a large, parlor-like room, in
an elegant residence away up town, on Madi-
son avenue. There was a long table in the

middle of the room, and every chair around the wall contained somebody who was waiting to see the doctor. Tom had been sitting down all day, and he was willing enough to stand and guess what was the matter with those people, but he kept his precious parcel tucked under his arm. One after another the doctor's visitors were summoned by a very polite, mysterious looking colored man, and passed on into an inner room, and nearly an hour went by, in spite of what must have been pretty rapid work in dealing with them. Tom stood on one foot then on the other, and he was still studying the patients when his arm was touched. The very polite, mysterious looking colored man had come for him, and he felt his heart beat as he followed. It was only through a door, into a small room where the doctor sat by a desk, bending over and writing something. By him, on the top of the desk, sat a black morocco case, that Tom thought he remembered. Instantly, off came the paper wrapping of the one he had brought, and, when the doctor looked up, there were two cases there, just alike, side by side.

"There it is, Dr. Harbeck," said Tom.

3

The doctor did not reply at once, but he picked up the returned case, opened it, looked sharply into it, and put it down. Then his keen, gray eyes flashed into Tom's and he asked: "Where did I leave it?"

"In the north elevator of the Probus building," said Tom. "I found it after you had gone."

"How did you know 'twas mine?" asked the doctor, with a quick, inquisitive look.

"There was no other doctor, all day," said Tom. "You came to see Mr. Angus, on the seventh floor. When you got in you had two cases—"

"Room two hundred and thirteen," muttered the doctor. "Did you know my name? Did you know that Mr. Angus was sick?"

"Not till afterward," said Tom. "I heard a man say you thought he'd get well."

"Humph!" said the doctor. "Don't tell anybody that he is sick, and nobody must know that he is there."

"I shan't say anything," replied Tom.

"I'll send out and stop my advertisements," said the doctor. "Now, what's your name?"

"Thomas Tracy. My father is janitor of the Probus building. But you haven't counted the money."

"I know it's all there," said Dr. Harbeck. "I'm glad you were so prompt. Glad you are honest. Honesty can't be paid for. Business-like promptness can be paid for. That's for the way you've done your business. Not one cent for your honesty."

He held out some greenbacks, as he spoke, but Tom hesitated.

"Take them," said Dr. Harbeck. "One per cent. on ten thousand. One hundred dollars. It's a straight, business transaction."

Tom's fingers ran over the bills with a queer tremor and tingle in them. Never in his life before had he owned more than a dollar at one time.

"I s'pose it's all right," he said, "but it's an awful lot of money."

"Promise not to spend a cent of it for sixty days," said Dr. Harbeck.

"I'll promise," said Tom, breathlessly.

"Then it won't hurt you," replied the doctor, as he turned and wrote rapidly in a memorandum book on the desk. "I want you to come and see me at the end of your two months. I wish to know how my prescription works."

"I'll come," said Tom. "I don't run the elevator, only to-day. It's my vacation, but I'm not going to school again."

"Yes, you will," said Dr. Harbeck. "You can't help it. You'll learn something all the while. Keep your eyes about you. Learn all you can. Go home now. Thank you for being so prompt. Come and see me. Good evening."

Out went Tom, not quite sure whether or not he had said good-bye, or anything else, but as he reached the sidewalk in front of the house he remarked, aloud:

"If Dr. Harbeck isn't made of lightning, I'd like to know what he is made of. One hundred dollars! It's the first money I ever earned, and I can't just see how I really earned it. Old Mrs. Cathcart's basket weighed a dozen times as much as Dr. Harbeck's case did."

He walked very slowly on his way to the nearest elevated railway station, for all the reasons for haste that he knew of were gone. He did not speak again of Mrs. Cathcart nor of the weight of her basket, but she had spoken of him several times

after he left her. She had wished that he
had gone all the way home with her, and
had been there to carry her baskets up
stairs for her.

"Grandmother," said the blind girl, as the
baskets were brought in, "Supper's ready.
Are you very tired?"

"Yes, Amy. It's a warm day. Busy, too.
They stole more of my oranges—the wharf
rats did—there, I won't speak of it again.
Poor dear! Alone all day!"

"All day!" shouted Crib. "Lone all day!
Great Crib! Hurrah!"

"I want a cup of tea," said Mrs. Cathcart,
as she sat down at the table; but Amy was
already bringing the teapot from the stove.
It looked as if she did not really need sight
to come and go, and to find at once anything in that room. There was another
room back of it, and two beds could be seen
in it through the open door. It was a
smaller room and seemed, like the larger
room, to have too much in it.

Amy took her seat at the opposite side of
the tea table, and her fingers seemed to find
without difficulty anything within her reach,
very much as if she were not living in the
dark. The canary sang in his cage, and the

parrot made occasional remarks. The glare
of the midsummer daylight slowly faded.
The supper was finished and cleared away,
and all the while Amy's grandmother talked
busily about a wide variety of matters.
She chatted cheerfully, even chirpily, but for
all that her face, which Amy could not see,
wore a deep, discontented kind of shadow.
Amy also talked, and asked, and answered
questions, and she, too, was cheerful, but it
almost seemed as if she were too much so.
It was a great deal as if each of them was
trying to make the other see how very con-
tented she felt.

About an hour passed by, and the shad-
ows all around the room were getting deeper,
when the one upon the old woman's face
changed into an expression of decision and
of business.

"Now, Amy," she said, "I'm going out
on an errand. I'll not be gone long. You,
and Pete, and Crib can keep house."

She did not say what her errand was, but
she picked up two of her baskets and hurried
away. She did not light a lamp before she
went, and it did not seem that Amy could
need one. When the blind girl was left alone,
however, the room was lonelier than it had

been in the day time, because Pete and Crib were now silent. The room had grown dark to them, and their bird bed time had come.

Amy attended to the tea dishes, and then walked hither and thither around the room, picking up things and putting them down again, as if she were making sure that they were all in place and order. Every chair seemed to have some particular spot upon which it was its duty to stand so that its young mistress could walk right to it and find it in the dark. No other person could have gone to and fro there as she did. People with good eyes could not have found their way without feeling for it much more carefully than she did. When all that was done, she went and sat down by the piano and played a little, and then she sang a very sweet, old-fashioned song, but she did not sing the whole of it. She stopped short, as if she did not feel like singing, and then she arose and once more walked restlessly around the room.

"I've heard them tell about prisons," she said to herself, aloud. "I feel as if I were in prison. I just can't stand it! It's real hard!"

The last words were uttered in a tremulous, plaintive tone, just as she came to the closed door at the head of the stairway. Her fingers felt for the knob and lock, and after finding them, kept their hold and turned and twisted.

"Open?" she suddenly exclaimed. "Has grandmother gone away and forgotten to lock the door?"

It was, indeed, open, and she stood still for a brief moment, in a kind of frightened, irresolute way. "I'll do it!" she said, in a voice which was almost a whisper. "I'll only walk down the stairs and up again."

It was a strong, masterful impulse, without any special cause that she could have given at that moment, but it led the blind girl down the stairs and out into the street. She walked out of a little world, of which she knew and could find every corner, into a great out-of-doors world, of which she knew nothing at all. She hardly knew what she had done. She heard sounds in all directions, but none of them were near her. There was no sound among them of a human voice. Her mind was in tumult and confusion, and her heart beat hard. For a minute or so, she walked along almost as if she could see.

Then she suddenly stood still, for a great feeling of fear had come upon her.

"Where am I?" she gasped. "Where is this place? Oh, it is all so dark!"

A million of people were around her, and yet she was alone—alone in the dark! There

"I'LL ONLY WALK DOWN THE STAIRS AND UP AGAIN."

was a boy walking along, just then, down a wide street which seemed almost deserted,

but which was all one glare of gas light and
electric light.   His hands were in his pockets,
and he was not even whistling, for he was
thinking.

"I can't get into the Probus building till
ten o'clock," he remarked. "Hello!"

Only a few steps in front of him stood a
bare-headed girl, in a light dress, holding
out her hands as if she were feeling for something that she could not find.

"So dark!" she said. "Oh, where am I?"

"She's blind!   She's lost her way!"
exclaimed the boy, excitedly, and he sprang
forward and caught hold of one of her
hands.

"Who are you?" she screamed. "Let
go! I want my grandmother!"

"Don't be scared," he said, very much as
if he were out of breath. "I'm Tom Tracy.
You're stone blind.   I'm awful sorry.
What's your name? Where do you live?
You ought to go right home!"

"I want to go," she said, reaching around
in a terrified way with her other hand. "I
want to get home right away. I'm Amy
Cathcart. Grandmother lives at the corner
of Garnet and Burgoyne streets."

"Oh, yes, I know her," said Tom, as if he were greatly relieved. "She keeps the peanut stand. She knows me. Now don't be so scared. I'll take care of you. Come along with me. How on earth did you get out here?"

"I didn't mean to," said Amy. "I just came down stairs to look around."

"Look around?" said Tom, and then he stopped and whistled, but she had told him the exact truth. She had been led out there by a blind girl's vague, feverish longing to see.

Tom was more excited than he had been by finding Dr. Harbeck's case in the elevator. He pulled Amy's arm into his and led her away, with a strong feeling that he was protecting her from all sorts of dangers.

"Here we are," he said, a few moments later. "Right up stairs, Amy. Oh, but ain't I glad you knew where it was!"

"Yes," said Amy, in a voice that still trembled a little. "I've always known the name of the streets."

"The stairs are awful dark," said Tom. "Can you find your way? I can't. Dark as a pocket. There! I forgot!"

For a moment he had actually forgotten her blindness, but she went up the stairs confidently and he went with her, and the door at the top was wide open.

"The room isn't lighted," said Amy.

"I'll scratch a match," said Tom. "I've got one. How did you know that the gas wasn't turned on?"

"'Tisn't gas," said Amy. "It's lamps. I can always tell when they're lighted. It makes a difference in the dark. It isn't the same kind of dark. I know when the sun shines and when it doesn't."

"Were you always blind?" asked Tom, as he lighted the largest lamp in the room.

"No, I wasn't," said Amy. "I stopped seeing all of a sudden when I was seven years old. I can think back now, and see some of the things I looked at before that. Since then it's all been dark."

Tom looked around for other lamps, and he seemed possessed to light them all, and then he plied Amy with an excited string of questions. She was more glad to have him there than she could have told him, and she mixed up a question of her own with every answer she made him. He said he would stay until Mrs. Cathcart's return, and he had no idea that he was being watched by anybody. He was just wondering what might be the color of Amy's eyes, if she should open them, when he was pretty sharply startled.

"Great Crib!" screeched a harsh voice, close to his left ear. "Hurrah! She's coming! Wharf rats! Peanuts, lady! Great Crib!"

CHAPTER III.

TOM AND THE MONEY KING.

THE screech which had startled Tom was hoarsely loud and piercing, and his face came round with a jerk, but he knew a parrot when he saw one.

Crib had been awakened by the light, and the chatter which had been going on had aroused him to action. He had hooked himself down from his perch, and across the floor and up the chair-back, until the top round furnished him with a first-rate holding. There he paused a moment, making motions with his beak which looked like a half-formed purpose of nipping Tom's ear, but his talkative tendencies conquered, and, instead of biting it off, he only sent his best voice into it. Part of what he said was instantly explained by a sound of feet upon the stairs, which he had heard before anybody else had, and in a moment more the door opened.

"Amy! Amy!" anxiously exclaimed Mrs.

Cathcart, hurrying in. "What is the matter? Tom Tracy!"

"Matter!" screamed Crib. "Matter!
Tom! He's a lubber."

The old lady had been astonished, on
reaching the street corner, by the unexpected
light that streamed from her own windows,
and she had made a breathless rush to find
out what it meant. She had left her baskets of fresh fruit and peanuts at the foot of
the stairs. She was now looking from Tom
to Amy and back again in a state of half
angry excitement, but her disturbance of
mind seemed to be nothing compared to
that of Crib. That brilliant bird was bal-
ancing himself on the chair-back and pouring
forth a noisy torrent of what he may have
meant for an explanation. After all, Tom
had barely escaped a hooked snap which
was aimed at the back of his neck as he
sprang up to meet Mrs. Cathcart.

"It's all right," he began, eagerly. "It's
all right! She didn't get very far away—"

"Tom Tracy!" exclaimed Mrs. Cathcart,
"Amy didn't get out, did she?"

"Yes, indeed, she did," replied Tom. "She
was away over on Broad street when I
found her. She didn't know where she was,

though. I brought her right home. She was scared half to death."

"Oh, dear!" said Mrs. Cathcart. "She's so helpless! And I've always been so particular about the door. She's never been out before, and hardly anybody knows where she lives, or that she's anywhere, at all."

She had to stop there and hug her granddaughter, who was now clinging to her in a way which ought to have calmed her down a little, but it did not. She talked right on and told Tom a great many things about the Cathcart family, the peanut business, and the great difficulty a lonely old woman found in caring for a blind girl. Tom heard it all without making many remarks, but he felt as if yet another kind of dignity were growing upon him. Not only he was a young man with money in his pocket, but he had found and rescued Amy, and had become her next friend and protector.

Mrs. Cathcart was full of gratitude, and she mentioned, several times, Tom's goodhearted conduct in carrying her basket, that afternoon, very much as if it had something to do with his finding Amy in the evening.

"Well, grandmother," remarked Amy at last, hugging her again, "ain't you glad it was Tom?"

It was as if he were an old and trusted friend of the family, and the one boy in New York by whom such a runaway should have been found.

"Great Crib!" said the parrot, gravely, but the talk went on without any reply being made directly to him.

"Tom," said Mrs. Cathcart, at last, "you've got to go home, now, but you may come again, some day, and hear Amy play the piano. She can play almost anything she has ever heard."

"Oh, but how I do wish I could read," interrupted Amy, as if her own thoughts had been going in a different direction.

"Read?" said Tom. "Don't I wish you could! And you could read music, too."

"That's what I mean," said Amy.

"I'll tell you what, though," said Tom, eagerly, to Mrs. Cathcart, "I'd just like to come and read to her. It would do her good. It's my vacation, and I can come as well as not. I'll bring a book."

The old woman stared at him as if his offer amazed her.

4

"Book?" she said. "You'll come and bring a book and read aloud to Amy?"

"Oh, grandmother," pleaded the blind girl, "let him come! I would so like to hear a book! Do let him come!"

"Tom Tracy!" said Mrs. Cathcart, doubtfully.

"Great Crib!" grumbled the parrot.

"Well, yes, Tom," slowly added the old woman. "I wouldn't let anybody else; but then—yes, you may come. She does get so awfully lonely. May be she'd really like to be read to. You can get the key of me at the stand. It's getting late now, though, and you've got to go home."

"I'll come to-morrow," said Tom, energetically, and then they said good-night, and he went out into the street with a strong feeling upon him that he had become a sort of guardian for Mrs. Cathcart's blind, orphan, and very helpless grand-daughter. It seemed to him that he had a great deal more than usual to think of as he walked along homeward.

There were lifting shutters, green wrinkles of steel bars, at the main entrance of the Probus building. They were the outer guardians of all the hundreds of doors inside, and of all the offices and property behind those doors, and the strictest care was taken that only the proper persons should pass them after certain fixed hours. Tom Tracy stood in front of them, at a little before ten o'clock, waiting for them to move.

"Boy," said an anxious voice behind him, "how am I to get in?"

"That's what you can't do," said Tom. "Not at this time of night. I can't get in myself till ten o'clock."

"Oh," said the stranger. "You belong here? I'm glad of that. My name is Gangway, Rufus Gangway, and my errand is of the utmost importance."

"They won't let you in on any account," said Tom. "What do you want? I'm Tom Tracy. My father is the janitor."

"I've got to go to room number two hundred and thirteen," said Mr. Gangway, still more anxiously. "All these papers, telegrams to be delivered,—must be!"

"Oh," said Tom. "They're for Mr. Angus. Well, nobody's allowed."

"Do you know he's there?" exclaimed Mr. Gangway. "You're just the fellow I

want to see. Tell me the truth, now. Can
he live? Is there any hope?"

There was almost a tremor in his voice,
and Tom's feelings were touched. He felt
that he could reply to that question without
betraying any secret.

"Mr. Angus is all right," he said. "Dr.
Harbeck says so. He'll be on his feet to-morrow."

"Hurrah!" all but shouted Mr. Gangway.
"That's good news! Best kind of news.
Can you take in these papers?"

"Of course I can," said Tom. "You
can't."

"Take them, then," said Mr. Gangway.

"Did you see Dr. Harbeck?"

"He was here to-day, and I've been at his
house this evening," said Tom.

"Boy," said Mr. Gangway, "it's the best
news I've heard in a long time. It's worth
thousands and thousands to me. Will you
give those things into his own hands?"

"I will," said Tom, and at that moment
a crack began to show at the bottom of the
shutters.

"Come in, Tom," called out the twangy
voice of old Kedzie. "Don't keep me waiting. That fellow can't come in."

" Tom," said Mr. Gangway, "don't let a living soul but Mr. Angus know I was here. Tom Tracy? Yes, that's the name. There, Tom, that's for you, but I'm thankful—"

"Come in, Tom," twanged Kedzie; and Mr. Gangway wheeled and walked off buoyantly, and Tom darted through the widening gap at the bottom of the shutters.

Kedzie's tongue ran right along, telling how strict were his orders from Mr. Tracy, about ten o'clock and those shutters, but Tom's mind was too busy for making replies. He shot up the broad stairway at once. That and all the halls and corridors were well lighted, although deserted and silent. On the third floor Tom paused, for a moment, to glance at the package of papers, and at the last thing given him by Mr. Gangway.

"I thought it was a dollar bill," he exclaimed, "and it's a ten! Well, I guess he knew what he was about. Those speculators don't care so much about a ten. I'll go straight to number two hundred and thirteen."

Up he went, story after story, and when he knocked at that door it was opened by a very sharp-faced, middle-aged gentleman, who only said, "Well?"

"Despatches for Mr. Angus," said Tom.

"Give them to me," said the sharp-faced man.

"No," said Tom, "I can't give them up to anybody but Mr. Angus."

"Give them to me," was responded in a harsh, imperative way. "I'm Judge Carpen ter. Mr. Angus is here. I'll hand them to him."

"No," said Tom, firmly. "I don't know anybody but Mr. Angus. I'm Tom Tracy, the janitor's son."

"All right, Carpenter. His head is level. Let him come in," called out a clear, hearty voice, inside, and the door swung open.

Tom walked in and saw a short, stout, gray-haired man, sitting in an armchair, by a table thickly strewn with papers. He seemed to be measuring Tom with his piercing, dark eyes.

"You know me, do you?" he said.

"You're Mr. Angus," said Tom. "Mr. Rufus Gangway told me to hand those to you. He went away."

"So!" remarked Mr. Angus. "Rufe hunted for 'em at my office, I guess, to get a chance to bring 'em. Well, well, my life or death is of great importance to Rufe. Did you tell him I am all right, Tom?"

"Yes, I did," said Tom, "but I didn't tell him all that Dr. Harbeck said when I was at his house. It wasn't much."

"Dr. Harbeck said little enough to me," interrupted Mr. Angus, with a sudden flash of interest. "Tell me what he said to you! Tell all of it!"

"He didn't tell me anything," said Tom, "but I heard him say to himself that Angus was safe this time, but he mustn't do it again."

"I rather think, then, that Angus won't," slowly remarked the great financier in the armchair. "That is warning enough. Angus will run away from overwork as fast as he can. Harbeck means that I must get away or die. Did you tell that to Rufus Gangway?"

"No, I didn't," said Tom, "but he understood, perfectly, that the effects of too much business and excitement threatened to kill the money king."

"Tom," said Mr. Angus, after a moment of thoughtful silence, "you have done pretty well. Keep your mouth shut about me.

There's ten dollars for not telling Rufe any more—"

"You can keep it," said Tom, proudly. "I haven't earned it. I don't want it."

The great man's manner had been very much as if he were dropping a crumb to a chicken, and Tom was feeling like a grown up man who had just made a fortune, and who had important business on his hands. Mr. Angus half arose from his chair, as if in astonishment.

"What?" he said. "Look here!"

Tom looked him straight in the face.

"Carpenter," said Mr. Angus, "look at him! He's a curiosity. I offered him ten dollars and he didn't take it. He'd never do for a lawyer."

Carpenter's sharp face was full of fun as he responded: "Yes, he will, though. No sound-minded lawyer would take ten when he could get twenty."

"But he can't," said Mr. Angus.

"Yes, he could," said Carpenter, "or a hundred times twenty, just for telling what he knows."

"I don't want your money," said Tom, reddening. "I'm not that kind of boy."

"You're right," exclaimed Mr. Angus. "Your name's Tom Tracy? I'll put it right down. I'll know where to find you, if I want you. Go along, now. I guess you can be trusted."

Out went Tom, and up the next flight of stairs, and the next, and on through the lighted corridors, until he came to the janitor's corner of the ninth floor. He knew that everybody there was already in bed, but he did not feel exactly like going to sleep. A great deal had happened to him that day, and he was in a flush and fever of excitement. He unlocked and opened a door, and the passageway he entered had in it a stairway not much wider than a ladder. At the top was a hatch that lifted easily on hinges, and in a moment more Tom was out upon the nearly flat roof of the Probus building. It was a splendid summer night, all stars and no moon. The salt wind that came from the sea was warm, and yet it made Tom feel cooler. He walked along and leaned against a chimney, and looked in all directions. All the streets of he great city, as he looked down upon them, were long lines of glittering lights. Every ship and steamer along the end-

less wharves, or at anchor in the harbor,
or in the bay, had lanterns hung out, to
keep other vessels from running into them.
Out upon Bedloe's Island shone the great,
blazing star that Tom called "the Liberty
Light," and away up the Hudson or "North"
River, and on the East River, he could see
the ferryboats coming and going like so
many floating illuminations.   It was a
grand place, up there in the silence, for getting a night view of the great city, and for
thinking.

"Why didn't I take that ten?" asked Tom
of himself.   "Mr. Angus has loads and loads
of money.   He could buy the Probus building and three or four blocks more.   I can't
guess how many.   Ten dollars isn't anything to him.   I'm glad I didn't take it,
though, somehow."

Tom was a pretty keen boy, but he
couldn't make it out.   It was one of those
points of honor which come to every boy,
but that no boy ever could "make out."

At that very moment, in room number
two hundred and thirteen, Mr. Angus picked
up a ten dollar bill which had been lying
upon the table.

"Carpenter," said he, "that is Tom Tracy's ten dollars, and I'm going to invest it for him and see if it won't grow a little. I couldn't take it back, you know."

"I guess it'll grow, if you take good care of it," replied the lawyer, laughing.

Tom heard nothing of that. He leaned against the chimney in silence, for a few minutes, and then he straightened up.

"I'll tell you what," he said, aloud, "I'll do as Dr. Harbeck said about that hundred. It'll take two months to know what to do with it, anyhow. I'll just lock it up and I won't spend a cent of it. I've got to speak to father about it, though. Guess I'll go to bed now."

Down he went, closing the hatch in the roof after him, and quietly found his way to his own room, and into bed, and he was asleep, like a healthy boy that he was, quicker than he might have expected.

The Probus building towered up to an uncommon height, but only a few squares distant from it there was another which was as tall but not as wide, and something interesting was occurring there at about this time.

The Australian building had also a wide entrance, in the daytime, that was now closed by folding, steel shutters, painted green. On the stone doorstep in front of them, sat something all curled up, and over it leaned a large man with a club in his hand. He was dressed in blue, with bright gilt buttons, and he had a yellow stripe on one of his arms.

"Get up!" he said, sharply. "What are you doing there? Get up!"

"OH, I BELONG HERE."

"Oh, I belong here," answered the curled up something, very sturdily.

"No, you don't," said the man in blue.

"Get right up. You're going to the station house with me."

"No, I ain't," came back, as the something began to uncurl itself, but its voice, this time, was not, by any means, so sturdy. "You're all right, though. You're Johnny Sample, the roundsman. I'm Gap Cruden, and they've locked me out. I didn't get home on time."

"Well, yes," said the officer, in a tone of deep and stern decision. "I know you. You'd ought to ha' got home an hour ago. I can't let you stay here. It's against orders."

Gap Cruden was on his feet now, and a more disconsolate youngster there was not, in all that ward of the city, during a long minute of argument which followed with that stony-hearted policeman. He did seem so awfully strong and cruel when his left hand closed with a grip on Gap's coat collar, and his right, with the club in it, pointed up the street in the direction of the police station—full of cells for arrested people.

CHAPTER IV.

TOM AND THE MONEY MARKET.

THAT was a dreadful minute for poor Gap Cruden, and he was altogether too badly scared to know that the merciless policeman who had griped him was really chuckling to himself all the time. Just as Gap began to feel himself pulled along and to shiver all over at the prospect of spending the rest of the night in a cell at the police-station, there was a metallic rattle behind him, and the green-wrinkle shutters of the Australian building were lifted a little.

"That'll do, Jack Sample," said a voice down by the doorstep. "I'll let him in. He'll have to go to the station, though, the next time he's late. I'm trying to teach him to be punctil. He never was punctil in his life."

"All right, Cruden," said the roundsman, "I'll let him off for this once, but he mustn't do it again. They'll send him up for ten days, on bread and water."

"Good enough for him," said Mr. Cruden, severely. "I told him to be in doors at nine o'clock, and here it is after ten."

"I got here at half past nine," whined Gap, as he stooped to crawl under the lifted shutters.

"That won't do, Gap," said the officer. "Half past isn't on time. Why, they'd turn me adrift, any day, if I should try and make 'em believe it was."

"That's so, Jack," said Gap's father, from behind his green-steel barrier, "and Gap's lost four places already, just by not being punctil. He's always got an excuse ready, too, but it won't work. Somehow or other, he's got to learn how to get in on time."

"Bread and water," chuckled the policeman, as he turned away. "He's the queerest kind of a little red-headed cub. I scared him good, but there's something else coming to him. Old Cruden had a rattan."

Gap had darted through the opening at the bottom of the shutters, and they came down with a click, so that neither Jack Sample nor anybody else outside of the Australian building knew whether or not

anything for punctuality was done with
that rattan.

If Tom Tracy had been awake at that
hour, instead of asleep, and if he could have
heard as far as Mrs. Cathcart's room, he
might have heard some words which interested Amy very much, as she lay and listened.

"Rent!" muttered the old woman, tossing
restlessly. "No, indeed! I won't pay those
fellows any rent, and they can't make me.
Amy's grandfather was born in this house,
and I was born next door. It's all hers, to
the next corner, if she had her rights. I
won't pay a cent to have her and me live
here, now, you see if I do."

"I never heard her say as much as that
before," thought Amy. "I do hope Tom'll
come to-morrow."

He intended coming, for the last thing in
his mind before he dropped asleep had been:
"What on earth'll I take to read to Amy
Cathcart? I don't know."

Gap Cruden did not get asleep right away
after his escape from being locked up as well
as locked out. He had seen a few inches of
the rattan as plainly as had the policeman
himself, and now he saw the whole of it, and
it seemed to recall unpleasant memories.

He also saw his father standing before him without any coat on and with his shirt sleeves rolled up.

"I—I didn't mean to be late," stuttered Gap. "There was some of us boys—"

The frown on Mr. Cruden's face did not relax, but he interrupted them in a voice that was so deep it cracked a little, trying to go deeper.

"Not another word!" he said. "Not so much as one word! Not one! Come along up stairs!"

There were a great many of those stairs, flight after flight, and Mr. Cruden seemed disposed to make the most of them. He took each flight a stair at a time, and each foot of the passages a foot at a time, walking slowly and solemnly a few steps in advance of Gap. He held the rattan in his right hand, and every now and then he struck with it smartly upon the wall, as he went along, or upon a stair above him.

"How that would cut, if it was me!" thought Gap. "He can just make it whistle. Ooof!"

He even thought more favorably of the station house, as they climbed the last story, slower still, and it occurred to him that

5

a cell might even be a kind of place of refuge.

The upper floor was reached, at last, and again Mr. Cruden turned and stood before his son in grim silence — very grim, indeed.

"I guess it's coming," thought Gap, as his father drew that long, pliant stick deliberately through the fingers of his other hand.

"Gap," said Mr. Cruden, suddenly pointing with the rattan very much as Johnny Sample had pointed with his club, "go to bed! I'll teach you to be punctil!"

Gap hurried away, oppressed by the weight of a desperate resolution that he would never again be behind time.

Tom Tracy's next thought came to him when the sun of the next morning, streaming in at his window, waked him up and pulled him out of bed.

"I don't want any elevator to-day," he exclaimed. "I must see about that, first thing I do." And then he added, more thoughtfully, as if he remembered another thing of importance: "Well, yes, all that money's there. I know it is, but I'd kind of like to take a look at it. I'll get my clothes on first, though."

It seemed to require some effort to wait, and even while he was brushing his hair with one hand, he unlocked the upper drawer of his bureau with the other and lifted out something.

"There it is," he said, as if he had been doubting it. "One hundred dollars, and it's all mine. I'm going to keep my word to Dr. Harbeck, though."

Back went the little packet of notes, and the drawer was locked again.

"Mother's getting breakfast," said Tom. "I'll go out and find father."

That, as he remarked to himself, was not always an easy thing to do, at that time of the day, for the great task of getting the Probus building ready for its business men was going forward under Mr. Tracy's direction. Perhaps he might have been harder to find if it had not been so very near breakfast time. Tom was walking along the corridor, studying in which direction to hunt first, when his question was answered for him.

"There he comes!" he said. "But how shall I tell him about it?"

Mr. Tracy came along with a brisk but

dignified step, as became the officer in command of the Probus business fort.

"Tom," he said, "no elevator for you to-day."

"I'm glad of that," said Tom. "Father, do you know how Mr. Angus is, this morning? Dr. Harbeck said he'd be better."

"How did you know that secret?" exclaimed Mr. Tracy, in a tone of utter astonishment. "Why, Thomas, it's all wrong! All wrong! The secret has leaked! How did it leak?"

Tom explained how he came to know about Mr. Angus, and his father listened as if he feared the management of the Probus building was breaking down.

"I'd no chance to speak to you about it last night," said Tom. "I knew you must know the secret."

"Of course I did," said his father, emphatically. "Every janitor has to keep secrets or he isn't worth a cent. Tom, keep your mouth shut, unless the building's coming down. Be careful whom you tell, even if it does."

"Oughtn't I to tell you everything, right away?" asked Tom, seriously.

"No, sir! By no means!" said Mr. Tracy. "Not unless it's necessary. I don't let anybody tell me anything, if I can help it. Have you got a secret, Tom?"

"Yes, I have," said Tom, "and it'll keep awhile, but I wanted to tell you."

"Don't you do it," was the almost stern reply of Mr. Tracy. "I'm bringing you up right. Don't you ever know a secret. If you do know one don't know it well enough to tell it. I've known lots of men to break up in business because they knew too much. Some break up because they told what they knew. A boy that can't shut up isn't worth a cent. Come! Let's go to breakfast!"

Tom stood in genuine awe of his father, and had great confidence in his good sense, but it helped him to be able to think: "Anyhow, it's two months before I need ask him what I'd better do with the money."

It did not so much as enter his head that he needed to say anything to his father about Amy Cathcart. Any advice upon that subject was to be looked for from somebody else than the commander of the Probus building.

Breakfast was the next thing in order there, and so it was in the second floor room on the corner of Garnet and Burgoyne streets. That room was full of an odor of coffee, and it was also full of Pete's morning music, as he swung in his cage at the window.

Mrs. Cathcart and Amy sat opposite each other, across the table which was continually inspected and remarked upon by Crib, as he cocked his head this way and that way and listened, knowingly, to the conversation. There was not a great deal of that, but at last, as the old lady arose, she exclaimed: "Books! Reading! I wish I had a boy like Tom Tracy to run my errands for me. There'd be some good in that, such a hot day as this'll be."

"Peanuts! Wharf rats! Hurrah!" shouted the parrot. "Oranges!" He continued to mention articles of her stock in trade, while she prepared her baskets and walked out with them.

The blind girl heard the key turn in the lock at the head of the stairs, and knew that she was shut in for the day. She felt better satisfied, after her evening's adventure, that the locked door was a wise precaution, but for all that the click brought back to her a doleful, imprisoned feeling. It was all the worse because of the fact that she had been actually out of prison, in the street, in the world, and had picked up a new acquaintance. And yet it grew easier to bear as she remembered that she was to have company.

That was a great thought, and a flutter of expectation grew upon her, as she attended to the breakfast things and then busied herself all over the room, putting it in good order. She seemed determined to touch every article it contained, as if to ask if it were in the right place and in condition to be looked at by company.

"I wish I could see him," she said to herself, aloud. "Oh, dear me! What if he should not come? He said he would. I do so hope he will come!"

The half dread that he might not seemed to make the room darker, or else Amy's eyes felt blinder, so strongly had she fixed her hope upon the promised visit.

"People have come to see grandmother," she had said, "but nobody ever before came to see me."

As for Tom he ate his breakfast, but he sat still until his father left the room. He did not really sit very still, and something seemed to be the matter with him, until at last it escaped at his mouth.

"Queerest thing you ever heard of, mother," he exclaimed, clearing his throat. "I have found a blind girl—"

"Found a blind girl?" said Mrs. Tracy, in great astonishment.

"Stone blind!" said Tom, and his portly mother stood in front of him, as he turned in his chair, while he rapidly went over the strange story of his meeting with Amy Cathcart.

He had questions enough to answer, but at last he asked one of his own: "Mother," he said, "you know more about books than I do. What had I better read to her?"

That brought Mrs. Tracy down into a chair, and the broom she had been holding fell upon the floor.

"Book?" she exclaimed. "I don't know."

"I've been all over the bookcase," said Tom, "but I can't make a pick."

Neither could she, for a while, but at last she made a suggestion.

"When I was a girl," she said, "I read Walter Scott's Lady of the Lake—"

"Poetry!" shouted Tom. "That'll do. Just the thing for her. She's blind."

What poetry had to do with blindness, in his mind, he did not try to explain, but his mother agreed with him. She had an errand for him, of her own, however, before he could be free to keep his promise with Amy, and he went down into the street to do it. He had just turned the first corner when somebody ran against him.

"Hello, Gap!" said Tom.

"It's you, is it," responded Gap, maliciously. "Lost your place in the elevator already, have you? Didn't know how to run it? Hey? Hey?"

"Look out that you don't lose yours," fired back Tom, and Gap dashed away, saying something about Strong & Bullard, and the great liking of that firm for punctuality. He did not tell Tom, nor anybody else, that he had thought more that morning about policemen and rattans than about all other things put together.

Tom finished his mother's errand and was glad, after that, that nothing seemed to call upon him to be in a hurry. He was aware of a curiously strong impression that he was a financial man, worth a hundred dollars, and that it was a very heavy thing to carry around. He walked along with his hands in his pockets, but he was carrying that money in his mind. He had several other things there, and they kept his mind busy until he found himself standing before the tall marble front of the Stock Exchange building. Streams of men were going in and out, and up and down the street, and they had an excited look. Tom knew that it was an excited kind of place, where riches came to men rapidly and went away as fast, and he was thinking of such things when a hand griped his shoulder.

"Hello, Tom," exclaimed somebody. "Come this way! How's Angus?"

"He's all right, Mr. Gangway," said Tom.

"Is he there yet? Of course. You've got to do something for me, and for him, too. The market's going all to pieces, and he doesn't know it. Take these papers to him and he'll understand it. They all say he's dead. I can't leave the street for a minute. Will you go?"

"Of course I will," said Tom, "but how does his death hurt the market?"

"Tom," said Mr. Gangway, "would you get around just as lively if your head was cut off?"

"I guess not," said Tom.

"Well," said the speculator, "Mr. Angus is the head of this market, just now. Don't you waste a second."

Off darted Tom, and he lost no time at all in reaching the door of room number two hundred and thirteen of the Probus building. It was opened, cautiously, by Judge Carpenter. Tom handed him the papers, and gave him Mr. Gangway's message.

"Come in, Tom," called out the voice of Mr. Angus. "Now, Carpenter don't show me one of those things on the table or tell me what they say. I mustn't look at any figures before to-morrow, but I know what to do."

"I'm glad of it," replied the lawyer, "for I must confess I do not!"

"Tom," said Mr. Angus, "go and call a carriage, and have it standing ready for me at the next corner beyond the Stock

Exchange. Go and tell Rufe Gangway to
meet me in front of the Exchange. Quick!"

"Carpenter," said Mr. Angus, as Tom
shot out of the room, "if two or three hundred men see me they'll all know I'm not
dead."

"Precisely so," said the lawyer.

Two other gentlemen were present, but
they said very little, and a few minutes
later there was a great buzz on the street.
The streams of men going to and from the
Stock Exchange saw the money king whom
they believed to be dead, and they saw him
walk briskly along until he met Mr. Rufus
Gangway. They seemed to greet one
another heartily, almost merrily, but other
people did not hear what they said.

"Rufe," said Mr. Angus, after shaking
hands, "you're not looking well. Why
won't you take air and exercise, my dear
fellow, and keep your health, as I do? I
don't mean to let business wear me out.
I'm dropping it."

"Just one moment, Mr. Angus," said his
friend. "A few words about that matter
of—"

"Not a word, Rufe," said the money

king. "I mustn't speak to a soul about business this morning. They must know I'm alive, though. Good-bye."

"Take care of yourself," said Mr. Gang-way, and Mr. Angus walked on rapidly to the carriage Tom had in waiting for him.

In that, as it drove away, he sank back as if he had done a day's work, for he was thoroughly tired out. Tom saw it go, but he knew nothing at all of the excitement in the money market caused by his errand to room number two hundred and thirteen.

When the money market of the great commercial city is disturbed, moreover, the effect of the disturbance goes all over the world, as rapidly as countless telegraphic dispatches can carry it. In the city where it begins, not only the stock market but every other market is troubled, and prices of wheat and hay and corn and cotton and other things go up and down, and so the farmers and planters, all over the land are made poorer or richer. Tom Tracy had not the least idea how many business calculations he had upset by bringing out Mr. Angus and showing him, all alive, to the men on the street, and he was in no way troubled

about the widespread disturbance. While
it was going on, and was extending over
the world, he was waiting by Mrs. Cathcart's peanut stand for her to give him the
key so that he could go and read poetry
to Amy.

CHAPTER V.

TOM AND AMY.

MRS. CATHCART did not let Tom have the key of her room until he had promised, several times, that he would bring it back again, and that he would not tell anybody about Amy. He felt very queer, indeed, when he walked away with that key. He was not at all ashamed of what he was doing, but not all the peanuts on her stand would have hired him to tell another boy, for instance, Gap Cruden, that he was going to read poetry to a blind girl. He left the old lady, and he walked along to the corner of Garnet and Burgoyne streets. When he got there he stood still for a moment, and looked up and listened. Not a sound was coming out of the open second story windows. Pete was not singing, because just then he was fluttering in his bath-tub, and Crib was watching Amy. She was sitting near a window, with a weary, disappointed,

yet eager look upon her face, leaning forward as if she, too, were listening.

"Great Crib! Hurrah!" suddenly shouted
her green-coated friend. "She's a lady!
Rats! Peanuts! Coming! Coming!"

Amy paled a little and trembled, for there
was a sound of feet on the stairs, now. In
a moment more a key turned in the lock,
and the door opened, and it seemed to her
as if the prison she lived in were a little
less dark.

Tom had felt sheepish, and bashful, and
doubtful, anything but confident, until he
stood in that doorway and saw Amy Cathcart's face as her hand went out to find him.

"Tom!" she said. "Is it really you, Tom?
Speak to me! Say something!"

He had tried to think what to say, and
had not found the right words at once.

"Yes, it's me. I've come, Amy," he
replied. "I couldn't get here any sooner.
How do you know it isn't somebody else?"

"Why, it couldn't be," said Amy. "It's
you. I know your voice. Oh, I'm so glad
you've come!"

"That's the book," he said, handing it to
her. "It's poems. I never read 'em, but

mother said it was the best I could bring."

"I know some poetry," said Amy, as her hands went over the book to get acquainted with it, but she could not see how red Tom's face was now getting.

His trial was right before him, and he was beginning to realize how terrific a task it was for a boy like him soberly to sit down and read any kind of poetry to any kind of a girl. He almost began to doubt whether he could do it, after all.

Amy opened the volume and her fingers went searching up and down the pages, but she did not say anything for a moment. She went back to her chair, and when Tom drew another up beside her she handed the book to him, and the parrot exclaimed:

"Great Crib!" as if in astonishment.

"It's the 'Lady of the Lake,'" said Tom, and the parrot responded, vociferously:

"She's a lady! Hurrah!" while Pete sent out an uncommonly loud trill.

"Read a little," said Amy. "I never heard anything about it."

Tom felt desperate, but he had come to read and he began in a somewhat tremulous voice:

"At eve the stag had drank his fill—"

6

"Tom," interrupted Amy, "what's a stag?"

"Oh, don't I wish I knew more about deer!" exclaimed Tom. "It's a kind of deer, and I've always lived in the city and there's none here. A stag looks like a,—well, if you saw one—"

"Yes," said Amy, thoughtfully, "it's a kind of deer. I saw one, once."

"Saw one! Did you?" exclaimed Tom, eagerly. "You didn't ever really see a deer, did you!"

"Yes, I did," she said, "and all sorts of other animals, and birds, and snakes;" and then, as he asked questions, it came out that she had been to visit a great menagerie, when she was a little girl, before sight left her, and that she could now recall the expressions of face of the smallest monkey in it. That brought forward another fact, that Tom Tracy had not failed to see every show worth seeing which had visited the city since he was old enough to go. So the "Lady of the Lake" had to wait until he had told Amy all he could remember, including giants, dwarfs, acrobats, and trained elephants. She asked and answered questions in an almost breathless excitement and delight, but her thoughts at last came back to the poem, and she told him to read again.

He opened the book and was about to do so when she put her hand on his arm and her closed eyes turned toward his face with a new inquiry.

"Tom," she said, "where did it all happen?"

"In Scotland," said he, with more than a little delight that he was able to say it.

"Where is that?" asked Amy.

Tom was a New York public school boy who had gone clear through a primary and grammar school. He could tell Amy things that she had never known about the face of the earth. He told several of them in trying to explain Scotland, and she was evidently thinking hard.

"Ships go there from New York," he said. "Steamers, too."

"Ships? Steamers?" she said, and then she clapped her hands. "Oh, yes, I can see them, now. I didn't right away, but I know what a ship is, and a steamer. The ships blow along over the water."

"I'll tell you all about them," said he, and on he went to do so, describing all sorts of vessels, as if he had made and sailed them,

instead of only seen them at the wharves or
in the harbor. The time went by faster
than they knew. At last he drifted back to
the book from an imaginary sail with Amy
in the bay, and she sat as still as a mouse
while he read page after page of the "Lady
of the Lake." He was still reading, and getting more and more interested, when a faint
sound of a steam whistle came through the
window, and then another and another, and
the parrot promptly responded:

"Dinner! Dinner! Great Crib! Hurrah!"

"Twelve o'clock!" exclaimed Tom, shutting the book. "Is it as late as that?"

"Must you go now?" she asked.

"I've got to be there at noon," said Tom.
"Father may want me for something after
dinner. Don't you eat dinner?"

"Nothing but lunch," said Amy. "So does
grandmother. We eat dinner at supper,
when she gets home."

"I guess I'll bring my lunch with me to-
morrow," said Tom, "and eat it here.
We'll read again, too. May I come?"

"Oh, do come!" said Amy, earnestly.
"I'll ask grandmother. It has all been so
wonderful!"

That did not mean the poem, half so much as it did the menagerie talk and the ships, but Tom was as eager about it as she was.

"Come?" he said. "I guess I will! I'll leave the book here."

She knew that he must go, and neither of them had much more to say about it. He shut the door behind him as he went out, and he locked it carefully, but that seemed a dreadful thing to do. He felt almost like a kind of jailer, but he was really in a hurry, and away he went. Amy listened until he was out in the street and then she turned and walked to the piano and sat down. She had forgotten all about it till that moment, and her fingers now only wandered over the keys. She struck a few notes and stopped.

"Oh dear me!" she said, "I wish I could hear some new music. Something I never heard before." After a brief silence, she added: "Yes, I can hear things and see things that I didn't know before."

She sat very still, there. It was the broad daylight of a summer noon, and she was sitting in the dark, in prison, remembering things she had seen and heard before the darkness came to her, and thinking of all that had been told her by her boy friend who could see. She did not know that he was a boy who really saw and heard more than did most other boys.

Tom did not linger at the peanut stand when he handed back the key to Mrs. Cathcart.

"I locked her in, safe," he said, "and I'm coming to read to her again to-morrow, if I can. I must go home now."

She was making change at that moment and he was gone before she could reply; but she remarked to herself: "I'd almost made up my mind not to, but it's just as well. She'll expect him. She's so lonely, poor thing!"

Tom reached the Probus building and went up to the ninth floor in the elevator, but he saw less than usual on the way. He was thinking almost too hard to see anything. When he reached his own dinner-table he was both glad and sorry, for his mother had company. He wanted to tell her about Amy, but he was not quite ready, somehow, and he was very glad she did not question him before his father and the three women who had come to see her. She looked at him and smiled and nodded, and he knew she wanted to hear, as soon as a chance came.

"Thomas," said Mr. Tracy, as he finished his dinner, "I want you, this afternoon, two o'clock till six. Side elevator."

"I'll be on hand," said Tom, and it occurred to him that he liked the idea.

A fellow could be all alone by himself in a packed elevator, and he could think as much as he wanted to. The visitors remained after dinner, and Mrs. Tracy was too busy with them to find time to talk with Tom. His own mind was so hard at work that he barely reached his post in the elevator on time.

Everybody else seemed to be uncommonly busy that day, for all the markets were excited, but Tom had no idea that he himself had done anything to stir them up or down. It seemed to him, however, that he had never before known so many people going up and down in that elevator. They were all in a hurry, too, and Tom was kept on the watch, stopping and starting his machine, but there would not have been an accident or an incident worth noticing, if it had not been for a piece of Gap Cruden's bad luck. The box was packed full, on an up trip.

"Tom! Tom!" he heard, from a husky, half choked voice, "lemme aout! Oh! it's the fe-ourth fel-lore! Oh! lemme aout!"

"Ho! what? The boy!" he heard next, in a very deep bass. "Colonel, you and I are smothering him."

"I can't stir," growled the colonel. "It's packed full. Jones, my boy, you're an awfully fat man!"

"So are you," said Jones. "There, bub, squeeze out."

"Lemme aout!" pleaded Gap, with a desperate kind of struggle to pass between them. O—oh!"

"Never mind, Gap," said Tom. "I'll let you out on the down trip."

"They pretty nigh buried me," said Gap. "If that biggest man had sat down on me, there'd ha' been a funeril!"

"I think there would, colonel," laughed Jones, but he handed Gap a quarter, and both of them got out.

Six o'clock came, and Tom went to supper, only to find that his mother was out taking tea with one of her friends, and that he was to go after her at nine. Kedzie would be ready to lift the shutters at that hour, and Tom was out of the building a little after seven, with only a dim idea as to what he had better do with himself. So he walked and walked, and let his feet carry him around among the deserted streets of the great city. Everywhere as he went, he looked up at the vast buildings, older and newer. He had been born and brought up among them, and he knew them all. None of them were residences except for janitors and their families. All were for business, of many kinds, and looking at them made Tom think of it, and of how much there was of it, and of the men who made and lost money by it. He was thinking of moneyed men, and of Mr. Angus and Rufus Gangway in particular, when he stopped in front of a very wide, high, plate-glass window, all one pane. He could look in, through a long, elegantly furnished banking-house office, with its safes and desks and chairs. All was clearly visible, even to what Tom knew must be the iron door of the vault where money and other valuables were stored. Not a human being was there and not a human being was near in the street, as he glanced around.

"That kind of door is hard to break in," he said, aloud, "but they could do it, if they had time. I've read of its being done."

He stood thinking of iron doors and safes and of burglars, when there came a heavy step behind him.

"What are you up to, Tom?"

All the boys in that region knew Mr. Sample, the roundsman, although few of them dared to speak to him. Tom turned at once and forgot all his awe of the grim official.

"It seems to me," he said, "that there ought to be more policemen. I guess some of these banks 'll wish there was, some day."

"Tom," said the policeman, "do you see that light in there?"

"I guess I do," said Tom.

"That's a police officer," said Sample. "Look all around, now. Bright lights in every office front. No burglar 'll work when all he is doing can be seen by everybody that goes by in the street."

"He could put the light out," said Tom.

"Could he?" replied the roundsman. "Well, you're a greenhorn! If the light in any of these places went out, that would notify the police to take possession of that place and find out what was the matter. There's an electric burglar alarm all over these offices that would send for the police if it was winked at."

"I wish I knew how it worked," said Tom, but the roundsman walked away.

So did Tom, and not a great while afterward he was on his way home with his mother, and she was asking him about Amy Cathcart. It was easier to tell about the blind girl, somehow, while they were walking, and Tom found himself giving all the particulars with enthusiasm.

"To think of her, there in prison all day!" exclaimed Mrs. Tracy. "Nobody to talk to! Only a canary and parrot!"

"I guess it is rough," said Tom. "I'm going there again, to-morrow, though. I want to hear her play the piano. I told her about every menagerie I ever went to. Mother, there's just one other matter—"

"Thomas," she said, "you get home and go to bed. I am going to see that girl, myself—"

She might have said more, but they were just in front of the Probus building, and it was nine o'clock, and the green steel wrinkles were slowly lifting. Anything else that was to be said would have to wait.

That was one of the safest buildings in the city. It had in it banks and banking offices, and safes and all that sort of thing, and it was fire-proof and burglar-proof, and it was also carefully watched; but it was broken into in an unexpected manner, right then and there.

Kedzie was polite, and the shutters went up so that Mrs. Tracy did not have to stoop uncomfortably as she and Tom went in. Kedzie had his eyes about him, watchfully, but he saw only those two. Nevertheless another form, all in white, flashed past him and went up the stairway as if all the police were after it. At the head of the first flight of stairs it turned and looked back for a moment, and then it darted up the next flight and the next, and was as yet all unseen.

The elevator was not running, and Tom and his mother had to work their way up on foot. It was a pretty warm piece of work, but Mrs. Tracy kept right on, bravely, to the third floor, before she paused for rest. It was an opportunity Tom had been waiting for, and he blurted out: "Now,

mother, that other matter,—father told me
not to tell him, but I do want to tell you.
You see, mother, I've made some money—"

"Money?" she exclaimed, as he hesitated. "Is it yours? How could it be
yours? Thomas!"

One glance into her flushed, troubled
indignant face, unlocked all the story of
Dr. Harbeck's case of surgical instruments.
He told it rapidly, and she listened with
intense watchfulness. When it was ended,
she drew a long breath, as of relief.

"Tom," she said, "I'm glad you took it to
the doctor right off. "I'm glad you didn't
take that ten dollars from Mr. Angus."

"Yes, mother," said he, "I'm glad, too,
but what had I better do?"

"You do just as Dr. Harbeck said," replied
she. "It's a good prescription. Look out,
though. Easy come is easy go. I'd twice
rather you'd worked hard for it; but it
can't be helped now. Come along up
stairs."

There was more than one more rest
before they reached the ninth story, and
almost all the rest of the way there was
half breathless talk about money, and honesty, and blind people, and neither of them

knew that the white intruder into the
Probus building seemed to keep only one
flight of stairs ahead of them.

They reached the outer door of their own
rooms, and Mrs. Tracy opened it with a
latch-key. The room within was lighted,
although Mr. Tracy had retired, that he
might be up at daylight in the morning.

"Mercy on us?" exclaimed Mrs. Tracy, as
that white shape flashed in between her
and Tom. "Where did that kitten come
from?"

"I know!" said Tom. "It came in with
us. I kind o' saw it, and then I didn't
see it. Isn't it pretty!"

He had sprung forward and caught it,
and the poor thing seemed glad to be cap-
tured. There was no ribbon, nor anything
else, to mark it, except a startlingly black
nose. All the rest of it was pure, spotless
white. There was no use in guessing where
it came from, but Mrs. Tracy remarked:

"We can't keep it here, Tom. What on
earth can we do with it?"

"Do with it?" echoed Tom. "Why I'm
going to take it and give it to Amy."

"Best thing you can do with it," said his
mother. "Give it some milk now."

He did so, while she threw off her bonnet, but just as he put down the saucer for the kitten, he heard his mother say:

"Thomas, show me that money! I can't feel just right about it!"

"I wish you would see it mother," said Tom. "I'd feel better. It's the first real big pile of money I ever had."

She went with him to his room, and she looked at the little pile of bills. She even counted it, and then she said:

"Well, I guess it won't hurt you, not if you mind Dr. Harbeck."

"Yes, mother," said Tom, "and I'll carry that kitten to Amy to-morrow."

He went to sleep with that purpose in his mind, but the real business of the next day began earlier for his friend Gap Cruden than it did for him. Not that Tom was not up first to give Amy's kitten more milk, but that he was not yet a man of regular business, like Gap.

The Australian building looked all the taller for not being very wide, and for towering several stories above a number of old, solid, brick and stone, three and four story buildings around it. Away up in the upper northeast corner of the tall edifice was a

small room which contained Gap and his
bed, and it was his duty to be up and out at
six o'clock.

All the clocks in the city were fairly punctual, that morning, although the sun was
more so. He waked up a great many people, just by coming. There was an alarm
clock in old Mr. Cruden's room, and it
banged away at six o'clock, precisely as it
had agreed to do when it was wound up.

It seemed, however, as if not one soul of
those who ought to have heard it had been
properly waked up, and no one was stirring
during the next quarter of an hour. Then
something of a stir did begin, and one of
the first symptoms of it arose in the room
where Gap slept.

"Yelp! Yelp! Yelp!" came in shrill and
anxious voices from a box in the corner of
the room. "Yelp!"

CHAPTER VI.

THE MASTIFF AND THE ST. BERNARD.

Gap Cruden's own private alarm clock had yelped for him and he sprang out of bed at once.

"York?" he exclaimed. "Boston? Wide awake, are you? Want your breakfast? So do I want mine—"

"Yelp! Yelp! Yelp!" was answered in a very beseeching manner.

Gap went straight to the box in the corner, and for some minutes he seemed to be much more interested in that pair of very small black-and-tan puppies than he was in getting dressed. They were, indeed, uncommonly queer little mites, full of life and fun, and Gap was having a real good time with them when he was interrupted.

"Gap! Gap! get up!" rasped a harsh voice. "You'll be late to breakfast!"

"They're growing, father," he said. "York's as big as Boston, but I hope neither of 'em 'll ever get any bigger."

7

"Drop those dogs!" was the stern reply.
"If you're late you won't have any breakfast. I'm going to teach you to be punctil."

A very queer, thin, big-headed, stoop-
shouldered man, was old Mr. Cruden. Another man once said that it made him stoop-
shouldered to carry so much head, and perhaps it was so. His own opinion was that
he carried too much responsibility, part of
which was Gap.

"He's gone," said the red-headed youngster to his pets. "I'll come back and feed
you as soon as I've had something, myself."

He was putting on his clothes in a hurry,
and some of them went on wrong side out
and had to be put on twice, but he was
really the quickest kind of boy in his move-
ments, after he got going.

"You're just in time, Gap," said a short,
thin woman, as he came into the room
where the rest were eating.

"Another minute, and your father'd say
you couldn't have a mouthful."

"No coffee for him," said Mr. Cruden,
severely. "I'll teach him to be punctil! I
can't stay a minute. Yah!"

There was a choking sputter in that exclamation, for a steaming cup had been handed him, and he had tried to swallow it in a hurry.

"Scalding hot!" he exclaimed, as soon as he could say anything. "O, my mouth, —Ha-h-h-h," and he blew breath after breath, but he drank no more coffee for at that moment a voice at the door said: "Mr. Cruden, it's after seven, and the Mountain Bank wasn't swept out last night, and the upper offices is like pig pens, and old Cromwell he said he'd hev to be here yurly, to-day—"

"I'm coming, Joe, I'm coming," replied Cruden. "It's enough to break a man down. Gap, I'll make you keep time or I'll know what's what. Hear?"

"Gap," said his mother, "do you hear that? You just escaped the rattan, night before last. Now you get ready and run an errand for me, and then you rush for Strong & Bullard's. Don't you be late there on no account!"

"Mother," said Gap, "I never am late. I wasn't ever behind time, not more than a minute or so. Sometimes their clock gets wrong, though."

"I guess the trouble isn't so much with their clock!" remarked his mother.

Gap finished his breakfast between telling about the tremendous rush of business at Strong & Bullard's, and about the iron severity of their dealings with their office boys.

"Well," said his mother, "if old Mr. Strong is that kind of a man, you look out for him."

He was hurrying away, just then, with a saucer of milk for his puppies, and when he returned she handed him a short written list of things that she wanted from a grocery.

"It's only a few blocks out of your way," she said. "Be quick about it."

"Mother," said Gap, "you just keep an eye on York and Boston. They'll get out and tumble down stairs if you don't."

"Those pesky puppies!" she exclaimed. "Well, I'll see they ain't hurt. Now, Gap, you just make time a-going."

There were not many people in the streets when Gap went out, and all of them were of the kinds that begin business early. Some of them drove carts, carrying supplies to the down-town restaurants, and the cart of an ice-man, coming up, met the cart of a butcher, going down, just at the corner below the Australian building. Right in front of the frosty cargo trotted a large frosty-looking dog, wearing a wire muzzle. A rod or so ahead of the butcher cart traveled a larger and very much fatter dog, with more wire on his head than was carried by the other. They did not wait a second, and the mutual dash they made only rolled both of them over and over, in a vain effort to bite, but the growling they did was really terrific.

Gap was standing by himself, on the corner when these dogs met.

"One's a mastiff," he said, "and one's a St. Bernard. Hear 'em!"

"Hear 'em!" echoed a voice behind him.

"Dog fight! Dog fight!" shouted another.

Gap heard other shouts and a clapping of hands, and a sound of much running in that direction, and in less than no time there was a crowd collecting. Down from his perch in front of his cart dropped the butcher, and out from his awning, behind his horses, jumped the ice-man, and each had a whip in his hand.

"Part 'em! Part 'em!" shouted the butcher.

"Give it to 'em!" growled the ice-man.

Gap sprang forward at that moment to be as near as he could and to see these dogs roll each other over, but he was not thinking how long a lash a whip might have if a fellow happened to be in the way. The next yelp did not come from the St. Bernard nor from the mastiff, although the second, and third, and several others did.

"Ow! Ow!" screeched Gap. "Yah!"

"Get out of the way!" roared the butcher.

"Clear the track!" snarled the ice-man.

Gap had obeyed them before they spoke, and in an instant more the butcher and the ice-man were getting back to their driving, while the dogs were trotting along in different directions. Gap hurried away in his direction, but he did not feel like trotting. He limped badly on his left leg, and he felt uncomfortable elsewhere as he made his way to the grocery. He felt excused, by his limp, for resting in front of a new kind of handorgan, and another minute in front of the grocery where a cart was putting down any quantity of cocoanuts, and when he got inside he stopped a little to rub himself, and to look at a pile of boxes of honey and then he handed in his mother's list, and set out for Strong & Bullard's office, in the Probus building, determined to get there on time.

The minute hand of the clock face on the tower of Trinity church was getting away from half past eight, when a red-faced, angry-looking man turned for the tenth time toward the door of the elegant office he was standing in. He slammed shut a great, heavy ledger with spiteful force.

"That boy!" he rasped, between his teeth. "Late again. I'll tell Strong! I won't have such a fellow 'round the office!"

Open came a door, and in dashed a boy in too great a hurry to remember which leg to limp on.

"You young vagabond!" greeted him.

"Mr. Curry, I started early enough."

"No excuses! I won't hear 'em! I'll report you this time."

"I didn't waste a minute, Mr. Curry," said Gap, pleadingly. "Biggest dog fight you ever saw! Mastiff! St. Bernard! Whoppers! Corner of Wall street!"

"Dog fight?" exclaimed the portly bookkeeper, excitedly. "How was it? Did you see them?"

"Mastiff, big as a calf," said Gap. "St. Bernard bigger'n he was. Ice cart, butcher cart, big crowd."

"Did they separate them?" anxiously inquired Mr. Curry. "I hope they did. It's inhuman, the pleasure some brutes find—"

"Oh, they parted 'em," said Gap. "Both of the dogs was muzzled. But I got hit on the leg with a whip. Hit me right here. Stung tremendous! Awful!"

"Well, Gap," said Mr. Curry, "seeing how it was, I'll let you go this time. Take that to the telegraph office. Quick!"

Gap did not lose his place that morning, therefore, but he made a beginning of an uncommonly hot and busy day, and running errands in the sun was hardly as pleasant as the work which seemed to be set before his friend Tom Tracy.

Tom's mother had had errands for him before breakfast, but before the middle of the forenoon he was ready to set out for the corner of Garnet and Burgoyne streets. When he did so he carried a small basket in each hand. The smaller of them contained a luncheon put up by Mrs. Tracy without consulting him, and the lid of the other was shut down over the black nose of a very angry white kitten. Tom did not tell the secret of either of these baskets when he obtained the key at the peanut stand, and Mrs. Cathcart could not ask him any questions, for she was waiting upon three customers at once.

That had been a strange sort of morning for the blind girl. Hardly was her grandmother away before she sat down at the piano. One bit of music followed another, as if they had been so many beads on a string. A number of them were mere fragments, worked out upon the keys very much as she had heard them. It was plain that they all were unsatisfactory to Amy.

"I don't really know anything," she said, at last. "There, that's all I do know. Tom won't care for it. He has heard plenty of good music. He told me he had."

She had no need to be ashamed of the music she had been making, and it was wonderful that she had picked up so much. After she had played it all, she sat still for a few minutes, and then another thought struck her.

"The dishes!" she exclaimed.

"Great Crib!" shouted the parrot.

"Dear me!" said Amy. "I must put everything in good order!"

She bustled around briskly enough after that, and nothing seemed to escape her. The breakfast things were washed and put away; the canary was cared for; the parrot was talked with in a way which accounted for much of his uncommonly good education; every chair was put into its place, and there was even sweeping and dusting done before Amy felt that she was ready for visitors. She grew brighter and looked happier while she worked, and now and then she stood still and seemed to look around her, but she was only thinking around and recalling the touches by which she knew all about that room.

"Hurrah!" screamed Crib, as if he knew she had finished it rightly. "She's a lady!"

She was not answering him when her lips opened, and she was not singing, but her voice went on in a very musical way. Without any effort to do so, she was repeating the opening stanzas of the "Lady of the Lake," just as she had heard them. Her ear had caught them perfectly, and there was nothing to prevent her memory from keeping them. The measure and the verse arrangement helped her. She was doing just as a host of people did in all lands, before printing was invented and when there was little or no writing.

"Hurrah!" shouted Crib. "Tom!"

The bird's ear had caught a new word and he was proud of it, and he repeated it again and again while the sound of Tom's feet came up the stairs. The key turned in the lock and the door opened.

"O Tom!" said Amy. "I'm so glad!"

"So am I," replied Tom. "I'm going to eat my lunch here, and we'll have a real good time. I've got the prettiest kitten—"

"Kitten!" exclaimed Amy. "Where is it?"

. "Here in the basket," he said.

"O Tom," she went on, "I used to have a kitten, and an old cat, too. I hope it won't run away."

"I guess it won't," said Tom, as he began to open the basket. "It isn't big enough to hurt Pete or Crib."

"That's what the old cat tried to do," began Amy, but he was putting the poor, frightened, white kitten into her hands.

"Oh, how soft and pretty it is," she exclaimed, as her gentle touch went over it.

"It's a Whitey," said Tom. "All white but its nose. That's black."

There was much to be said about Whitey, and about the mystery of his getting into the Probus building after hours, but Amy's mind had been pretty full of another business when he came in.

"Now, Tom," she said, "let's have some more reading. I remember all you read yesterday."

"Remember it!" exclaimed Tom, in astonishment. "I don't remember ten words of it. I thought it was pretty good, too."

He picked up the book, nevertheless, and colored a little, and hemmed. and began where he had left off, while Amy seated herself to listen, with Whitey in her lap.

"Great Crib!" said the parrot. "Tom! Hurrah!"

Half an hour or more went by, and the expression of Amy's face followed the meaning of the poet's words remarkably, but she seemed to be almost hard at work listening, and she grew tired.

"Now, Tom," she said, "don't read any more. I've got to play for you before you go."

She arose and put down Whitey and went to the piano, while Tom was saying: "That's just what I wish you would do."

He also took a chair and went and sat by the piano, and it was his turn to listen.

"You do play splendidly!" said Tom, the first time she paused. "I don't see how you can do it. Go on!"

"I don't know many more things," she said, "except what I make up. I wish I could hear some more."

"Play all you know, and all you ever made up," replied he, with enthusiasm. "You've just got to hear another lot, somewhere. Mother's coming to see you, and she and I can fix all that."

"Can she, Tom?" said Amy, almost feverishly. "Can I hear more music? O Tom, Tom, I'd be so glad!"

"Of course you can," he said. "Why, there's loads of it. Mother and I'll take you to hear some, right away."

The parrot kept still while the piano was going, but he had remarks of his own to make whenever it ceased.

"I guess he's fond of music," said Tom, at one of the noisiest pauses.

"I do believe he is," said Amy. "That's the way he always acts, but grandmother says he's an Irish parrot."

"Did she buy him of an Irishman?" asked Tom.

"No," said Amy, "but some Irish sailors gave it to her, and they'd taught him everything they could think of. Now, listen."

She touched the piano again, and it was a tune Tom had not heard before, but the moment it began Crib's feathers bristled.

"Great Crib!" he exclaimed. "Hurrah! Murder! Rats! Peanuts!" And then, as the tune went on, he broke out into a series of discordant screeches, mixed with words that neither Tom or Amy could understand. They may have been Dutch or Spanish, for all Crib told them.

"Don't you see?" said Amy. "It's 'God Save the Queen,' and he won't have it. It's the only tune that makes him screech."

Screech he did, whenever he heard her begin it, and she and Tom were laughing at him when the steam whistle blew for twelve o'clock.

"Now for lunch," said Tom.

"I'll make coffee," replied Amy.

"I'll help, and we'll see what's in the basket. Mother didn't tell me, but she's the best kind of cook."

"Is she fat?" asked Amy.

"Well, no," answered Tom, "but she isn't thin."

"I thought all good cooks were fat," said Amy. "Grandmother says she can't cook, but that I can, and so I'll be fat, some day."

Amy was entirely serious in that impression, and she was also very curious about the contents of the basket.

"Ham sandwiches," she said, as her fingers touched one.

"Great Crib!" screamed the parrot. "Peanuts! Bananas! Oranges! Cocoanuts!"

"Sponge cake," said Tom, "and some cold chicken. We'll go out and have some ice-cream, some day, if your grandmother 'll let you go."

"I don't believe she will," said Amy.

"I'll get her to let you," said Tom, "and mother 'll just make her."

The coffee was now ready, and Amy was more than proud of the array she knew the luncheon was making.

"I can almost see it," she said, "and I'm glad it's such a fine tablecloth. It's one we had before I was blind. There are whole trunks of things. Some of them are away in the bedroom."

Tom had already heard, in several shapes, that Mrs. Cathcart had not always been poor. There were things in those rooms that poor people do not buy, and the tablecloth was better than any his own mother had.

He and Amy ate their luncheon, and then she positively refused to let him help her wash the dishes.

"Now, Tom," she said, when that was done, "I don't want any more poetry, but it's too bad you can't stay all day."

"I don't want any more, either," said Tom. "I wish we had something else."

Just what to talk about he could hardly think, and it was of no use for Crib to make suggestions; but the tablecloth did better, and the talk went back over that to things that Amy could remember, long ago, when she could see.

"It was a high house," she said of the house she had lived in. "It was red."

"That's brick," said Tom.

"And there were three flights of stairs, and ever so many rooms, and carpets and furniture, and a piano, and pictures. I can think of it all, and then it goes away into the dark and I can't see it."

Amy was trying hard to remember something more, when they were interrupted.

"Great Crib!" shouted the parrot. "She's coming! She's a lady! Hurrah!"

Crib had not blundered, for a step was on the stairs, and Tom hurried to the door and opened it.

"Mother!" he exclaimed. "O Amy! Mother has come to see you!"

"Tom," said Mrs. Tracy, "your father wants you, right away. Don't wait a moment. I've come to send you home and to see Amy. Why! My dear girl! O,—yes, —dear—"

"I'll go right along, mother!" said Tom. "You can leave the key at the peanut stand. Good-bye, Amy."

"Good-bye, Tom," called Amy. "I want you to come again, as soon as you can."

She said it without turning her head, and Tom did not wait to see what it was that had so startled his mother. Amy had walked straight up to her, as if looking in

8

her face, and Mrs. Tracy had put out both hands to help her come, but Amy had not taken them. Her own hands glided right over those of Mrs. Tracy, up her arms, and then had paused upon her face, as if searching for something she wanted to find. Amy's lips were parted, and she was breathing very quickly.

"You are Tom's mother," she said.

Just then she discovered how hard a real mother could hug, for Mrs. Tracy's arms went around her, and Amy was squeezed and kissed again and again.

"My poor dear!" said Mrs. Tracy, "I am so glad I came! Dear child!"

"I'm so glad, too," said Amy, once more touching Mrs. Tracy's face, and something was there that moistened the tips of her inquiring fingers, but the blind girl did not know that Tom's mother could not help crying.

The hug was finished, and then Mrs. Tracy looked at everything in the room, from the stove and dishes to the furniture and the piano, and Pete in his cage, and the flowers and plants. Great Crib called her Peanuts, and told her she was a lady.

As for Tom Tracy, when he left his mother
and Amy and hurried to the Probus building, he found that something entirely unexpected was waiting for him.

"Two o'clock, Thomas," said his father,
when they met, on the ninth floor. "You've
just fifteen minutes to get to Mr. Gangway's
office."

"Why, did he send for me?" asked Tom,
with a twinge of astonishment. "What
does he want me for? O dear! There goes
my vacation!"

"I'm sorry about that," said his father,
"but he's a good man to work for. Anyhow, go and see what it is."

Off went Tom, obediently, and, as he went,
the thought of his vacation melted swiftly
away before a growing ambition to get into
business.

"What can it be!" he said to himself. "I
just wish I knew what was coming."

CHAPTER VII.

TOM AT SEA.

AMY CATHCART grew more and more delighted with Tom's mother as they went around the room and talked about all sorts of things, and she decided also that Mrs. Tracy was quite fat enough to be a good cook. After a little while the piano was once more set a going, and Crib's Irish prejudices were again aroused for the amusement of his new visitor. Mrs. Tracy asked all about Tom's reading, and she was as surprised as he had been over the blind girl's memory.

"I'm glad you like poetry," she said, "but you don't want that all the while. I'll have him bring you something else next time he comes."

It seemed real hard work, at last, for the good woman to get away, but she had to go. Amy clung to her to the very door, and made it harder yet to be firm and say "Good-bye," and then it seemed positively dreadful to shut the door and lock it carefully, and take out the key, and leave Amy shut in there all alone. Mrs. Tracy went down the stairs, saying to herself:

"It is too bad! I'm going straight to see that old woman!"

In a few minutes more she was at the peanut stand, telling the story of her visit with Amy, while Mrs. Cathcart silently pulled the papers from a whole dozen of oranges.

"I don't know about it," said the old lady at last. "She'll be getting discontented. I'm glad your so kind.—Peanuts? Yessir. Five cents worth.—Tom's a good boy. I'm glad you're his mother. Oh, yes, I've seen you before. Well, yes, Mrs. Tracy, she may go to the Probus building with you some day. You'll take good care of her. She'll need a hat, but I've no time to get anything for her—"

"Leave that to me," interrupted Mrs. Tracy. "I'll see about her hat. I must go home now," and off she went.

"I almost guess it's time Amy did know somebody besides me," said Mrs. Cathcart to herself, after Mrs. Tracy walked away, "and I can't let any of the other people around there speak to her."

She was evidently much troubled about it all, however, and she caught herself making mistakes in change several times within the next few minutes.

Mr. Rufus Gangway's office was in the Australian building, away back on the lower floor, and he was sitting behind his desk when Tom came in.

"Got here, have you?" he quietly remarked. "Your errand will be ready for you at half past two, precisely. You can leave word at home that you're not likely to be back early."

"All right," said Tom, as he sat down; but it seemed a little odd, for he was not yet in Mr. Gangway's employment, and here was an errand and an order.

Fifteen minutes went swiftly by, and toward the end of them he saw the busy financier arranging a packet of papers and putting them into a long envelope.

"There, Tom," he said, "I've heard Mr. Angus' opinion of you. You're the right boy to send. You can keep a secret."

"Where is it to go?" asked Tom, for the envelope bore no address.

"That is what nobody must know," said Mr. Gangway. "He is on board his yacht, the Rover, and she's off Pier Two Hundred, South Brooklyn. That letter's for the captain of the yacht. Angus forgot it was here, probably. You can deliver it to him. Hand that envelope only to Mr. Angus himself. Come and see me to-morrow morning. I'll know what to do then."

Tom Tracy felt that confidence was being placed in him. He was almost too proud to speak, and he did not ask a solitary question, but he took the packet and the letters and walked out of the office. His first errand was to the Probus building, and to his father.

"Back again?" said Mr. Tracy. "What for?"

"It's Mr. Gangway's directions," said Tom. "He's sent me off on a long trip. Can't say how long it'll take. Private business."

"Keep it private, Tom," said his father. "Don't tell me a word more'n you'd ought to. Honor bright, Tom."

"I guess I understand," said Tom, and he stood very straight when he said it.

"Off with you," said Mr. Tracy, but Tom hurried to his own room, first.

Mr. Gangway, in his haste, had forgotten to provide even car fare and ferry money, and Tom decided to take plenty of both from the drawer where he had stowed away his capital.

"Not from the hundred dollars," he remarked. "Only from the ten. Mother isn't back from Amy's yet."

Down the elevator he went, with his ten dollars in his pocket.

"Hello, Tom, where are you go'n?" inquired Gap Cruden, as they met at the bottom.

"China or Japan," said Tom, as he dashed past him.

"Wish I was there," said Gap, "so I was out of Strong & Bullard's. They need a steam boy."

It is not a long distance from Wall street to the southerly shore of Brooklyn, but it seemed so to Tom, for he had never before made the trip, and he felt that he was upon important business. He had to go by a ferryboat which left Manhattan Island, or New York city, from the battery, or from the site where there was an Indian village once, and where the Dutch and then the English had a fort. It looked as little like it now as Hendrik Hudson's ship, the Half Moon, would have resembled Mr. Angus' yacht, the Rover, that Tom Tracy was on his way to find.

A very beautiful schooner-yacht, indeed, was the Rover, and she lay at her wharf, when Tom Tracy reached it, with the air of a vessel that would much rather have been doing something else than lie there. Any sailor would have said so, at all events, for her crew were on deck, her sails lay loosely along their booms, and everything was ready to move at a moment's warning. Tom himself knew enough about such things to understand so much, for he said to himself:

"I guess Mr. Angus is ready to go. He's only waiting for his papers."

A narrow gang-plank rested between the Rover and the pier, but Tom was halted when he put his foot upon it.

"What do you want?" asked a sailor, gruffly.

"I want Captain Andrews," said Tom. "A letter for him. And Mr. Angus, too—"

"I'm Captain Andrews," sang out a bronzed, decided-looking gentleman, coming

forward quickly. "Come on board. What
is it?"

Tom crossed the plank and handed him
the letter, but not the packet, in spite of the
hand held out to take that also.

"I can't give that to anybody but Mr.
Angus himself," he said, firmly.

"All right," said Captain Andrews, after
reading the letter. "Come down with me
into the cabin."

Tom followed the gentlemanly sailor with
a thrill of pride and with a sudden feeling
that he was exceedingly fond of the sea,
himself, and of ships, and that the Rover
was exactly the boat that he would like to
own, and command, and sail on. He did
not take note of a few graceful motions
which Captain Andrews made with his
right hand, as he turned to his crew, just
before going below.

Tom and the captain disappeared. The
sailor who had halted Tom, trotted off
upon the pier and cast loose the hawser
which held the Rover there. That done, he
pulled in the plank which carried him back
on board while all the other hands hauled
vigorously upon the mainsail and up it

went, catching a fair westerly breeze as it did so.

"So you must see Mr. Angus," said the captain, as he and Tom entered the luxurious cabin of the Rover.

"I can't give up this to anybody else," said Tom. "Important papers."

"Right! You're right!" exclaimed the captain. "You'll know him when you see him, if I go on deck and leave you here?"

"Oh, yes!" said Tom. "I know him."

"Of course. Of course," said the captain. "And they can't expect you home right away."

"They don't," said Tom. "They won't be worried."

"I'm glad of that," said the captain. "Wait here a little. I've got to go on deck."

"Certainly," said Tom, but there came to him a strange, a very strange sensation as the captain disappeared.

"He locked the door behind him!" exclaimed Tom. "The Rover's moving! Hear them on deck! What does it all mean? I wish Mr. Angus would show himself. They'll have to put me ashore—"

If he had been on deck, just then, he would have been deeply interested in what he saw. The great, white wings of the Rover were fully spread, and her smaller sails were fluttering out, one after another. Everything had, indeed, been in perfect preparation for a prompt send-off. The swift, graceful, beautiful craft seemed to rejoice in getting free from a pier and a snubbing-post. She was sweeping away from the shore at a splendid pace, while Tom Tracy sat in the cabin, on an elegant divan, waiting impatiently for Mr. Angus.

"Maybe he's asleep in one of those state-rooms," he thought, "and they don't want to wake him up. I've got to wait for him, but I'd rather be on deck than down here. Isn't this elegant, though? It must have cost piles of money."

There could be no doubt of that, for the Rover was a floating palace, so far as its fitting up was concerned. She was also a bird of the sea for speed, and she went over a long stretch of salt water during the quarter of an hour which passed before Tom again had company.

Mr. Angus did not come, even then, but

Captain Andrews, as polite and as smiling as at first.

"Tracy, you said your name was? Tom Tracy?" he asked, as he took a seat and looked into the now somewhat anxious face of his boy passenger.

"That's it," said Tom, "and I'd like to see Mr. Angus and go ashore."

"You know Mr. Angus?" asked the captain. "And he knows you?"

"Oh, yes!" said Tom. "I've had business with him before this."

"Then I think I'd better let you read that," said Captain Andrews, holding out the letter Tom had brought to him. "You can't deliver your other errand to any hands but his, and I'm going to take you straight to him."

Mr. Gangway must have been altogether in the dark as to the contents of the letter to Captain Andrews which had been sent to his office to be forwarded by him to the commander of the Rover. Tom read it, now, and the part most interesting to him was in these words: "Take the Rover around to New London. I will meet you there. On no account let any soul on shore know that I am not on board."

It was signed by Mr. Angus!

"Captain Andrews!" exclaimed Tom, in amazement. "Do you mean to say I've got to go all the way around Long Island before I can see Mr. Angus?"

"Splendid sail," said the captain, with a cheerful laugh. "We'll treat you first rate. I'm glad to get out of harbor, myself. Come on deck, now, and have a good time."

Tom sat very still for a moment, and there was a queer feeling in his throat and along his waistband.

"I guess you're all right, anyhow," he said, with a strong effort to speak as if he were entirely satisfied.

"I'm all right, am I?" laughed the captain. "Come up, my boy. Come right on deck and play sailor. You can deliver that thing to Mr. Angus, at New London. You are going to find him before anybody else will."

He got up as he spoke, and Tom followed him on deck and looked around and aloft. It seemed to him as if he never had had so keen a sense of being alive as that which came to him while he looked and realized his very extraordinary situation. With all her sails set, the saucy Rover was dashing across the lower bay toward the narrows. She was on her way to the open sea,—to the Atlantic ocean,—and Tom Tracy was her only passenger. It was almost as if she were his own, for that trip.

"At sea!" exclaimed Tom. "I'm at sea! I never was out at sea before. It's the biggest kind of thing. Hurrah!"

The hurrah sounded hushed and low-voiced, for Tom was under a heavy pressure of excitement, but his checks were flushed, and his black eyes were sparkling with pleasure.

"I'm really glad you like it," said hearty Captain Andrews. "We'll have an out-and-out good time."

Long before Tom Tracy came up out of that cabin, a red-headed and red-faced boy dashed into the office of Strong & Bullard, somewhat as if he had reached them at the end of a hard run. He had nevertheless, arrived either a little too late or a little too soon, somehow.

"Peanut shucks! Orange peel! Banana skins!" he heard, growled out in the deep husky voice of the head of the firm. "What has become of that boy?"

"I didn't waste a minute, Mr. Strong," said Gap, in an anxious tone, as he held out a sealed envelope. "I had to wait for 'em to give me that answer."

"I didn't say you hadn't," grumbled the gray-headed banker. "What's all this mess on the floor? Do you mean to make this office a pig sty? Get a broom! Clear it up!"

"Twasn't there when I went out," began Gap, as he went to a corner and searched for a broom which was also not there.

"Come here, sir," said Mr. Strong. "Turn your side pockets inside out."

Gap's face grew dreadfully red, but he silently obeyed. One pocket had in it nothing but a handkerchief, a strap and buckle, some string, two lead pencils, a piece of rubber, and some business cards, but the other produced a sensation. It was a bulging pocket when Gap began upon it, and it was full of danger.

"Bananas!" exclaimed Mr. Strong. "Pretty near a pint of peanuts—"

A roar of laughter from the bookkeeper and the others interrupted him.

"That'll do, Gap," said Mr. Strong. "You hadn't eaten your peanuts. Somebody else did this. I'll let you off. Take that tele-gram. Quick, now!"

Off he went, and when he returned to the banking office it was empty.

"Narrowest kind of get off," he said to himself. "I did eat some of those peanuts. I've got to look out what I do with my shucks."

Mr. Tracy was feeling uncommonly well satisfied concerning his son that after-noon.

"My dear," he said to his wife, "it's a good thing. Mr. Gangway is the right kind of man for Thomas to be with."

"But where's he gone?" she asked.

"Private business, my dear," he replied, almost reprovingly. "Do you s'pose I'd let him tell me? A boy with a leaky mouth isn't worth a cent."

"But, husband," she said, "he ought to be back in time for supper."

"Supper!" said Mr. Tracy. "What's his supper compared to his business? He must learn not to care too much for his supper. A boy that thinks about eating, when he's got something else to do, isn't worth a cent."

9

"I do wish I knew where he'd gone," she persisted. "I had some things I wanted to say to him."

"About that there blind girl?" he responded. "Nonsense, my dear! Tom, reading poetry to her, instead of 'tending to business? Fudge! Humbug! I'm sorry she's blind. Of course I am. Of course you are. Of course he is. Humph! A boy of his age that takes to reading poetry isn't worth a cent."

As for Tom himself, he was just then sitting upon a coil of rope, near the heel of the Rover's bowsprit, as she dashed through the Narrows. He was staring eagerly at the grim walls of the forts and at the embrasures from which the great guns peered out, when Captain Andrews came and stood by him.

"Having a good time, Tom?" asked the captain.

"Tip-top," said Tom. "I guess any British man-of-war that tried to get in here would get all it wanted."

"I guess it would, if it was one of their big iron-clads," replied the captain. "It would get the forts, popguns and all, and

then it would steam in and get the city.
Yes, it would get all it wanted."

Tom's countenance fell, for he had been
brimful of pride and patriotism concerning
those forts. They were so grand, so
magnificent, with such lots of cannon. He

"I'M REALLY GLAD YOU LIKE IT."

could not believe that they were really old-
fashioned affairs, which could not do much
hurt to a new-fashioned enemy.

Captain Andrews seemed to feel worse
about it than Tom did, and went on into a

kind of free lecture about war ships and armor, and forts and cannon and torpedoes, and all that sort of thing.

"Now, Tom," he said at last, "come down with me and get some supper. You'll have one of the forward staterooms to-night."

Tom arose from his coil of rope, but in a moment more he sat down upon the deck. Nobody else did so, for the captain and the sailors had their sea-legs under them, and were used to the motion of the Rover.

"Up with you," laughed the captain. "She's going lively. We're going to have the liveliest kind of night, or I'm mistaken."

Tom got up and followed him, with a clear idea of the difference between a deck and a sidewalk. Never in his life before had he made a voyage upon any craft less steady than a ferryboat, or over waves that amounted to anything. He was conscious that he was getting excited about this boat and these waves, however, and he determined to play sailor as well as he knew how. Down they went, to a prime good supper, in the cabin. Tom ate with a hungry boy's appetite, while Captain Andrews proved that a prime good sailor can beat a hungry boy.

"Now, Tom," he said, after answering kindly no end of questions about yachts and other vessels, "you may come on deck and take all the comfort there is going. Don't fall overboard, that's all. I'll see to it that you hand your papers to Mr. Angus. Have a good time!"

Tom went out on deck, just as the Rover was pitching heavily in the deep wake of a vast ocean steamer.

"She's one of the biggest of the Cunarders," said the mate, when Tom spoke to him. "She's British. There isn't a Yankee steamer a crossing this old heaving pond. Yonder's a German, and we passed a Frenchman a little while ago."

That was another rub on Tom's patriotism. Ship after ship and steamer after steamer swept by the Rover, as she dashed away into the wide waste of the Atlantic. The breeze freshened, and the spray came flying across the deck. The staunch craft leaned over, at times, in a manner that startled Tom, in spite of his faith in the seamanship of Captain Andrews.

"What's he running so fast for?" he ventured to ask the mate, as the dusk of the twilight began to settle over the water.

"He wants to get a good offing," said the mate, gruffly. "He's right about it, too. We're in for a rough night."

It was like an unknown tongue to Tom until he had asked more questions. Then he knew what an offing meant, and that the worst place in the world for a sailing vessel was anywhere near shore, in a gale of wind, unless it blew her away from the land.

"And you can't count on that," said the sailor.

Deeper and deeper grew the gloom over the ocean, the white crests of the waves gleaming through it in a way that made Tom feel serious, but he kept up his lookout. He saw the sailors hang out their brilliant lanterns, and then, far and near across the sea, he could shortly discover other twinkling points of light hung out by sailors on other craft.

"We're going to have a rough night of it, are we?" he said to himself. "That means that there's a big storm coming. I don't care. Let her come!"

CHAPTER VIII.

THE CRUISE OF THE "ROVER."

THE lights upon the ocean which Tom Tracy was watching from the deck of the Rover, as she dashed on before the strong wind which was driving her, were of vast importance to a host of people. Just as they began to glimmer, at yardarms and at mastheads, the street lights of the city flashed out in quick succession. The gaslights, wherever they were, did nothing without help from a torch or a match, but the electric lights had an appearance of knowing for themselves the right time to kindle, and then to kindle on their own account. There was a burner of that sort in Mrs. Tracy's sitting room in the Probus building, and when the time came it made so sudden a jump into brilliancy that it startled her. She had been sitting very still, looking out of a window toward the harbor, and when the little glass bulb near her flashed into a glow of white light she put her hands before her eyes and exclaimed: "O Tom! where can he be?"

She was not the only person who seemed to have that question in mind, for Mr. Gangway, arising from his dinner table, remarked to another gentleman: "No, sir, I hardly expected him back soon enough to report to-day, but I shall see him first thing in the morning."

There was enough of light, away out at sea, for Tom to watch the sailors of the Rover, as they took in sail after sail. The smaller sails, that he did not know by name, came in first, until only one narrow jib remained, while of the larger sails, only the mainsail, reduced in size by reefing, now caught the increasing pressure of the wind that was blowing. It was worth any land-boy's while to hold on hard by the rail and see those spreads of canvas come in, and hear the orders, and to see how perfectly the men did their work. Tom had heard Captain Andrews remark, too, that sail had been kept on quite as long as was at all safe, and he knew that a long distance had been put between the Rover and the shore of North America.

The wind itself had not been reefed or diminished, but it had changed its direction. It had been westerly, to blow the Rover out through the Narrows, but it kept veering around to the northward until it went too far, altogether, and was rapidly becoming what the mate described as "a nor'easter."

"They never last long, in midsummer," added Captain Andrews, "but there's enough of one of 'em while it's blowing."

Tom knew they were talking of what was yet to come, but he was strongly of the opinion that there was quite enough of that nor'easter already.

"Time for you to go below, Tom," said the captain. "I'll help you get there safe and sound. You can read or do anything you please, but I can't let you stay on deck any longer."

"I guess I'd rather be down stairs than up here," said Tom. "Is it really going to storm much harder than this?"

"I guess likely it'll blow some before morning," said the captain. "You go to bed and sleep. She won't roll as badly as a steamer would. You'll have a real good time."

The Rover was a capital sea-boat, and her motion was not so very unpleasant, in spite of a rough sea that was rising fast, but the wind and waves together were making a tremendous racket. There were papers and magazines and books in the elegant saloon which Tom now had all to himself, but he could not compel himself to read one of them. The best of them could not have contained a chapter half so interesting to him as was the chapter of actual experience which he had been trapped into by Mr. Rufus Gangway's sly attempt to find out whether or not Mr. Angus were on board the Rover.

"It's the biggest thing that ever happened to me," said Tom to himself. "I wonder what mother'll say, and father, when I tell them. Won't they open their eyes? I'm sorry for one thing, though. Amy'll look for me to-morrow, and I can't come. I'll have something better than poetry to talk about when I do see her, anyhow. I'll go to bed."

Amy had not forgotten him, although her mind had been pretty full that evening. Mrs. Cathcart returned from her hot day of business in a disturbed state of mind,

although peanuts had sold well. She had
almost been cross to Amy, and had refused
to answer several unusual questions which
Amy had asked her about men and women
and things that she said she thought of, as
if she remembered them, away back long
years ago, before she was blind. That
was early in the evening, and Amy was still
busy around the rooms, setting matters to
rights, as if her desire to keep things in
order was growing upon her. She must
have had something else upon her mind,
too, for at last she exclaimed:

"There! I don't think I know what that
part of it means, and so it won't come back.
I can repeat all the rest. It's real nice to
know it, and to say it over and over."

She had not repeated aloud what she
knew of the "Lady of the Lake," but she
was looking triumphant over the idea that
she could once more astonish Tom Tracy
by remembering so much.

"It makes me think of all those other
things, too," she said, "and I can see them
better than I used to see them."

Amy was silent after that, and so was
her grandmother, and so was the parrot,
except when a sharp gust came through the

window, and all but swept him from his perch.

The windows had to be quickly closed, but the gust there was nothing at all to the one which roared around the ninth story of the Probus building. The windows went down there also, and by one of them sat Mrs. Tracy, staring out into the darkness and saying, again and again:

"It's of no use, Mr. Tracy, I can't have him sent on errands that keep him away from home all night."

The absent boy she was thinking of sat in the cabin of the Rover for some time, listening to the tumult of the storm and to the sounds which came down now and then from the deck. At last he began to feel almost ashamed not to go to bed.

"If Captain Andrews should come down and find me up," he said to himself, "he'd say I was scared."

That thought drove him to his stateroom and into his bed, but he hardly intended to go to sleep. He was pretty tired, however, and his eyes soon closed. They remained shut until the Rover tacked, and then he suddenly found himself wide awake, and grasping wildly out for something to hold on by.

"She's tipping over," he exclaimed. "No, she isn't! What is it? I hope it isn't going to be a shipwreck."

He heard a great sound of cracking and roaring, but he had listened to something like it before he went to sleep, and after a few seconds he could remember it better.

"I wish I were on deck!" he almost groaned. "If she is sinking, they ought to let me know. The cabin door is locked, too, and I couldn't get up stairs. What would mother say if she knew where I was! O dear!"

Tom felt peculiarly until the steadiness of the Rover's plunges into wave after wave reassured him a little. He did not know that even the captain and the mate, on deck, were remarking that it was well for all on board of her that the Rover was "a good sea-boat." She rode the water well, and she was well handled. Gust after gust swept her swiftly onward, and each fierce rush of wind seemed stronger than that which went before it. Tom Tracy's eyes closed again, after his first determination to try and be still, and he did not know

what it was which once more made him
open them. Neither did he have an idea
how long his second nap had lasted.

"It's almost as dark as a pocket in here,"
he said, "and I couldn't tell if it was morning. I'll get up, anyhow."

Getting up was not so hard a task, but
standing up was harder, and there seemed
to be no such thing as finding his clothes or
putting them on.

"I know where I left them," he said, "but
I want more light—there!"

He had worked his way to the door of the
stateroom, and opened it. The lamp that
hung in the cabin had been turned low, but
it was still burning, and he could see that
everything which had been loose when he
first went into it had now been put away.

"There isn't anything that can roll
around much, except me," remarked Tom,
three seconds later as he climbed upon a sofa
across the cabin. "That was awful sudden.
She isn't wrecked yet, though. What would
mother say!"

The Rover was steadier for several minutes, and he managed to dress himself.

"I wish I had a watch," he said, and just
then the cabin door opened.

"Hello, Tom," said the voice of Captain Andrews. "Up and dressed, are you? Did you sleep any?"

"Oh, yes," said Tom, putting all the courage he had into his face and voice. "But isn't it time to get up?"

"You might as well stay up," said the captain, "but it won't be daylight for more than an hour."

"May I come on deck and see the storm?" asked Tom, very much as if he were fond of storms.

"I guess I can take care of you," said Captain Andrews. "Come along. Hold hard! There's a wind blowing."

Tom thought so, but then he was not a sailor, and he knew very little about wind.

"This can't last long, captain," said the mate.

"I hope it won't," said the cool commander of the Rover. "She's as dry as a bone below. We'll weather this gale in good order."

"'Tisn't so dark up here," said Tom to himself. "There are not many clouds. I can see stars now and then. What waves! She isn't wrecked yet."

Not yet, but he saw for the first time the difference between having waves around a ship, and a ship floating like a big cork on the side of a wave. The next thing he learned was the difference between a wave breaking against a ship, and a wave broken into by a ship, nose first, or rather, bowsprit foremost. The Rover was built to go over water rather than through it, but she seemed to make a complete dive into that gigantic billow.

"Hold hard all!" he heard the captain roar through his trumpet, and he griped his rope desperately.

Oh, how he did hold on as that flood of salt water swept the deck! He felt that he was away down under it, and his thoughts flashed through his mind like lightning.

"Is she sinking? Am I drowning? Will she ever come up again? Mother won't know I'm drowned! I can't breathe! Oh—oh—yes, I can! Phew! Whish! It chokes me—"

That was because he tried to catch his breath too soon as the waves went by and let him out, and the next thing he heard was a round of cheers from Captain Andrews and the sailors, for the way the Rover had had gone under and come up again.

"I'm awful wet," said Tom. "Don't I wish I were at home again!"

He had hardly spoken before he heard yet another sound. It was like a sharp scream at a distance, and it was followed by loud exclamations from Captain Andrews and his men. He could understand only a little of what they said, but his heart beat hard.

"Going down!" he exclaimed. "What a pity! Some other ship is wrecked worse than we are!"

"Captain Andrews," shouted the mate, hoarsely, "her light was more 'n half a mile to windward."

"She's foundering!" roared the captain. "There goes her light!"

"Gone down!" groaned the mate. "And we can't do a thing!"

Tom himself had caught a glimpse of the light which disappeared, and he strained his eyes eagerly in a hope of seeing it again, but it was of no use. Some craft that was not so good a sea boat as was the Rover had plunged under an ocean surge and had not come up again.

10

The next thing Tom understood was the great grief of Captain Andrews that he could do nothing for men who might possibly yet be swimming, for the Rover could not sail against the wind.

"I wish she were a steamer, just now," he said. "No use to send a boat. It'd be swamped in no time."

The men offered to go, but he refused to take the responsibility, although he tacked back and forth in a sort of vain hope of saving somebody.

"No use," he said, again, at last, and then the Rover dashed on her course.

She went through several big waves, but when Tom managed to speak of them to the mate, he was told that all this was nothing to the dives the yacht had made while he was down in his stateroom.

"She's a reg'lar duck," said the mate, "but the wind's letting up a little, and it's pretty near daylight."

Less and less fierce grew the puffs of the gale, but the waves were still chasing each other with tremendous energy when the glow of morning began to spread across the sky. Tom was almost surprised to find how thoroughly the wind had dried him.

He felt chilly, too, until the rising sun had warmed him up, but after that he grew more comfortable, and tried to study out the problem of how every tack the Rover made, in seemingly opposite directions, brought her so much nearer to Montauk Point, at the easterly end of Long Island. He was thinking of that, and of the ships whose sails were visible between him and the horizon, when Captain Andrews hailed him.

"Well, Tom," he said, "I guess you're feeling better, now. No more storm on this trip. We'll land you in New London to-morrow morning, sure!"

"I'm glad to hear that," said Tom, with energy, "but, oh, ain't I hungry!"

"I guess so," replied the captain. "Come along. Breakfast's ready."

Just about that time, away up in the ninth story of the Probus building, a stout lady was fussing around the kitchen with a look of extreme dissatisfaction upon her face.

"My dear," said a voice at the door of the room, "'t isn't time to get breakfast."

"Mr. Tracy," she said, "Thomas may

return at any moment, and he shall have his breakfast as soon as he gets here."

"I guess he'll eat his breakfast somewhere else," said Mr. Tracy.

There was yet another stir among Tom's city friends, but this one was at the bottom of a building, not at the top. The sun rises earlier in mid ocean than it does in the deeply shaded streets of a city of tall houses, and it was the racket of carts, rather than anything shining, which stirred up motion in a bundle of clothes upon the doorstep of the Australian building. It was a bundle which Jack Sample, the roundsman, may have overlooked purposely, and now it stretched a leg, and then an arm, and then it sat up.

"Locked out!" came from under the straw hat it picked up and put on. "If this isn't the meanest place to sleep in, I wouldn't say so! I'm awful hungry, and there isn't a place open yet, where I could get a mouthful."

He sat still a few moments, and then he rose and walked up and down, and looked peculiarly unhappy. He did not notice a slight sound at the entrance near him, but the steel shutters lifted slowly, and a woman's face peered out under them.

"GAP, YOU BAD BOY, * * * HAVE YOU BEEN THERE ALL NIGHT?"

"Gap, you bad boy," she said, sharply, "you come right in, this moment, and get something to eat. Have you been there all night? You're a bad boy! Why didn't you get home on time? You're never punctual!"

"Mother," he said, as he came hastily forward, "I wasn't more'n ten minutes late, or fifteen, and it's the meanest place to try and sleep in."

He dodged under the shutters, just then, and they began to close down, but his voice came out through all the opening left.

"Poor fellow!" she said. "Sleeping on a stone! It's dreadful! You'll never be late again, will you? Poor boy! Served you right, too. You're hungry! Come right along and get some breakfast."

"Mother," said Gap, "I just do promise I'll never be behind hand again, as long as I live. I did think I was going to get here."

"Gap," she interrupted, "your father's waiting for you, up stairs."

Just there the steel shutters came all the way down and no more could be heard outside.

CHAPTER IX.

"YORK" AND "BOSTON."

THAT day was Sunday, but there was no church door open anywhere near Tom Tracy. He ate a hearty breakfast in the cabin of the Rover, talking with Captain Andrews about storms at sea and shipwrecks. Then he went on deck and for some reason or other he never so much as thought of getting seasick. He was now not only dry, but fairly comfortable. He had taken off his wilted collar, as being no longer of any use, and he had smoothed his clothes as well as he could, but he was aware that they were somehow a great deal tighter in their fit than they had been the day before.

"She's running fast, anyhow," he said, as he looked around him.

"We'll reach New London to-morrow," said the captain, cheerfully.

Now that Tom was beginning to feel at home on the deck of the yacht, there was no end of enjoyment in watching the waves and in looking for the distant sails of other ships and for the trailing smoke of steamers. They were almost as plentiful as wagons upon a much traveled road. Tom tried hard to think only of those which were afloat and in motion, but now and then he could not help remembering the great cry he had heard in the dark, and the light which had disappeared beneath the stormy water.

"I'll never forget that as long as I live," he said to the mate.

Then he thought of his mother, and he knew that she must be getting ready to go to church. She was; and she was just then saying to her husband: "This afternoon, Mr. Tracy, I'm going to go and see that poor blind girl. Tom would like to have me; I know he would."

"Go and see her, my dear," he replied.

"It's an awful thing to be blind. Tom's eyes are as sharp as needles."

There was a pretty serious Sunday morning in the top story of the Australian building. Gap Cruden was listening to a continuous lecture on punctuality, from his father, and all the while he had two other things on his mind. He thought of his night on the stone slab, and that thought helped his father's lecture amazingly, but he was also thinking of the sad fact that on reaching his room he had found no traces of two little fellows who should have been there. Both York and Boston had mysteriously disappeared, leaving not so much as a yelp behind them, and the lecture came to a sudden end when Gap mustered courage to tell the news.

The dog question became at once a family matter, and it troubled old Mr. Cruden every bit as deeply as it had troubled Gap.

How could any thief, however cunning, have evaded all the safeguards of the Australian building and carried off two black and tan puppies?

"They couldn't have gone down by the elevator!" exclaimed Mrs. Cruden.

"They never left home of their own accord," remarked Gap. "But if they did get out, and if they've been out all night, they'll never get back again."

"I'm afraid somebody's been a loafin' 'round," said Mr. Cruden. "Come along; I must make a thorough search for them."

"We're coming with you," said Mrs. Cruden. "Come, Hannah! Come, Jane!"

She said that to a pair of elderly ladies from the country who were visiting her, and in a minute more they were all marching in a procession, with Mr. Cruden at the head of it, carrying bunches of keys in his hand. He wore a solemn and important look, for he was the only man entrusted with the opening of all the doors in the Australian building.

"York and Boston couldn't have let themselves in anywhere without a key," said Gap, "and I don't believe they fell down stairs."

Room after room of the upper floor was opened and examined, and in every one, Mr. Cruden found fault with the way in which things had been left.

"Fact is," he said, "we were a little late in getting at it, last evening, and a heap of work had to be left over. We'll have to be a going early, to-morrow. We've got to be more punctil."

There were no dogs on that floor, and before the one next under it was finished the entire party was getting not only warm but excited. Gap did most of the active searching under desks and lounges and behind boxes, all the while whistling and calling the names of his lost favorites. His father, on the other hand, seemed to have an idea that black and tan puppies were likely to get into fireproof safes, for he carefully tried the door of every safe, as he came to it. That was one of his habitual duties, as janitor, but then, no kind of puppy, not even a clerk or an office boy, was likely to know the secret numbers of a patent combination lock.

"I don't like the look of things," said Mr. Cruden, as they went down the next flight of stairs. "I'm going clear through the whole concern."

If it had been the Probus building, he could not have done it, but there were fewer rooms here, and the women now began to help Gap, vigorously.

"Not a dog to be found," whimpered Gap, when they reached the lower floor. "There's been somebody snooping for 'em. Any number of fellows would like to have such a brace of puppies as they are."

"It's a serious matter, my son," groaned Mr. Cruden. "Anything missing from this building would be the ruin of me. I'm glad it's only dogs this time."

The banking and insurance offices on that floor were really splendid affairs, and Jane and Hannah said so, and they almost forgot about the puppies while they stared around in one room after another.

"There's nothing left now," said Mr. Cruden, "but Mr. Rufus Gangway's office. He hasn't let any dogs in, but he was here mighty late last evening."

He threw open the door, as he spoke, of a spacious room in the rear of the building, and they all looked in.

"There's lots and heaps o' money been made and lost in this 'ere den," began the old janitor.

"Yelp! Yelp! Yelp!" responded to him from somewhere behind the mahogany railing which guarded the inner two-thirds of the office. It sounded almost like "Yelp me! Yelp me yeout of this yere."

"York!" shouted Gap. "Boston! York! Boston! where are you?"

"Yelp! Yelp us yeout!" they replied, as he darted forward to find them.

"Here they are, father!" shouted Gap. "But how did they ever climb into this 'ere waste-basket?"

That was, indeed, a problem, for the willow wicker-work, though only a foot in diameter, was four feet high. There was a thick mass of waste paper at the bottom of it, and that had been the bed of York and Boston. It had been softer than Gap's limestone slab, but they had had no breakfast, and they said so.

Mr. and Mrs. Cruden and Jane and Hannah guessed at how they got in, while Gap was lifting them out, and he made his own guess as he hugged them.

"It must have been one of the boys," he said, but right here he was startled by a loud exclamation from his father.

"The safe's open! Maria! Gap! Mr. Gangway's safe door is open!"

"Husband!" said his wife. "Hannah! Jane! The same man that stole the pups has been robbing Rufus Gangway!"

Mr. Cruden had thrown open wide the huge, double doors of the fire-proof, burglar-proof, ponderous mass of chilled iron and steel, and its precious contents of account books, papers, and packages of securities, and of nobody knows what, were exposed to view. He stood looking at it for a

moment, and then bang went the safe doors
again.

"Wife," he said, "bring me a chair. I've
got to sit right here until Gap finds Rufus
Gangway and brings him to search this 'ere
safe. Gap, you go right along. Don't you
come back without him. I'm glad you did
sleep on the doorstep last night. Travel!"

"Mother," said Gap, "you take the puppies. I'm off."

"Hannah," said she, "take that one.
Jane, you take that. I'll get a chair for
him."

Gap vanished; the chair was brought, and
Mrs. Cruden and her two friends shortly
began a weary climb of stairways, groan-
ing over the fact that the elevator did not
run on Sundays. They left behind them, in
Mr. Gangway's office a gray-headed, under-
sized man, faithfully leaning back against
the closed doors of a great iron box, and
very deeply regretting that he had neglected
his duty of trying the lock of it as soon as
the office was closed on Saturday evening.

Mr. Cruden had given Gap the street and
number of Mr. Gangway's house, but time
had gone by since breakfast in that long
search for lost dogs. It seemed to Gap, too,

that even the elevated road was a slow affair, and he got to the house only to be told that Mr. Gangway was already at church.

"St. Giles', did they say?" he said, as he darted down the steps. "I know where it is. I'll get him!"

It was not many minutes before he was whispering awful news to a ponderous sexton in a church vestibule. A minute later Mr. Gangway, in his pew, listened to another whisper, a loud one.

"Message from the 'ous, sir! You're wanted at once, sir! The safe's been robbed, sir!"

"You don't say!" replied the financier, and half the congregation turned their heads to see how swiftly he went down the aisle to the door.

He learned all there was to be learned from Gap, and he learned it pretty coolly.

"Go and get me a carriage," he said. "Tell your father I'll come at once and bring others with me. There are millions in that safe. Serious business!"

Off went Gap on that errand, and as soon as it was done at a livery stable, he set out for home. When he got there the shutters were raised by Mrs. Cruden.

"Mother!" said Gap, excitedly, "it's all right, he's coming. Did you feed 'em?"

"Your father's 'feared there's been a robbery," she gasped. "It isn't his fault if there has been, but he'd lose his place for not trying the door, last night. Oh, dear me! And he so punctual, too!"

Gap's question had referred to York and Boston, but he was in a hurry to make his report. He went right in and told what he had done, while his father sat like a statue, or as if he were a part of the safe door.

"'Tend the entrance, Gap," he said. "Nobody's agoing to get into this safe while I'm alive."

He looked as if he meant it, and the stern expression did not leave his face even when Mr. Gangway and his bookkeeper, and three other gentlemen, who had trusted precious things to that huge iron box, came anxiously into the room.

"Glad of your vigilance, Mr. Cruden," said the great speculator. "I wish we'd known this last night, though. That's where your mistake was. How it came so is a mystery. Try the door, Beckwith."

The bookkeeper tried it, and it opened as if it had no lock at all.

"Not locked," he said. "I locked it. Somebody else knows the combination. We are robbed, beyond a question."

"Count everything in it," said Mr. Gangway. "Count at once."

Mr. Beckwith, of course, had a list of everything that should have been there, and every article was compared with that list as it came out. They had reached the end of it when Mr. Gangway said, reading from the list: "Ten gold certificates, of ten thousand dollars each, one hundred thousand dollars."

"Not here," replied the bookkeeper. "I did not have them."

"Stolen!" exclaimed Mr. Gangway.

A brisk discussion followed, but all that was understood by Gap or his father was that ten precious pieces of yellow-looking paper had in some manner disappeared.

"I guess the pups didn't get 'em," said Gap, but Mr. Cruden was grimly silent.

"No suspicion of blame rests upon you, Mr. Beckwith," said Mr. Gangway, "but we must clear the matter up. They would

11

easily have gone into a long envelope without crowding it."

They were all excited, but they all kept their tempers, and Mr. Cruden felt better to hear them say positively, at last, that the missing treasure must have been left outside of the safe.

Gap was glad when he got a chance to slip away for a visit to York and Boston, and the last words he heard were from Mr. Gangway: "Those gold certificates belonged to Mr. Angus. What can have become of Tom Tracy?"

There was no one to tell him, and he was not the only person on shore who was hourly becoming more and more interested in that question.

Mrs. Tracy gave up expecting her son to come home to breakfast, and both she and Mr. Tracy were more silent than usual while they were getting ready to go to church.

At the corner of Garnet and Burgoyne streets everything was at first very quiet that Sunday morning. The rows of carts remained at the curbstones, and no horses or drivers came for any of them. The small shops were all closed. The dingy old houses

"IT HASN'T BEEN OPENED FOR YEARS AND YEARS."—Page 176.

also looked as if the people who lived in them were disposed to sleep later than usual. Old Mrs. Cathcart did, for she had been very tired on Saturday evening, but her blind granddaughter did not. She knew when morning came, and she arose with the coming of the sun. Every article of any consequence in the main room had to be visited and touched before she seemed entirely satisfied that it was still there. She fed her feathered pets, and then she lighted the fire · in the little stove and began to get breakfast. Just a moderate clatter of the dishes, while she was setting the table, awoke Mrs. Cathcart, but even after the old lady came out and sat down to her coffee, she seemed to have very little to say. It was a very quiet place, indeed, until a while afterward, when Amy sat down at the piano. The moment she struck a note, the canary followed her example, with all his might, and the parrot joined in after his own fashion, until a kind of storm of mixed music poured out through the open windows.

"I guess Tom won't come on Sunday," said Amy, as she ceased playing, and both Crib and Pete closed their mouths, while a faint mew from Whitey died away and left a complete silence.

"No," said Mrs. Cathcart, "of course he won't."

Even in church, Tom's mother several times said the same thing to herself, and she was fidgety to the end of the service. When it was over, however, and on her way out of church, and on her way home, she spoke to several other women about Amy Cathcart, and her blindness, and her music, and her need of a new bonnet, and of new dresses, and of other things. They all expressed the deepest interest, and promised to come and see about it. Mrs. Tracy herself went to see about it very soon after dinner. She was heartily welcomed, especially by Crib, but he spoke vigorously of peanuts, while Amy's first questions related entirely to Tom, and the answers she received were anything but satisfactory, although his mother assured her that he would soon be at home again. The impression left on Amy's mind, after all, was only that Tom was away out in the great, dark world, somewhere, and nobody knew exactly where.

"Poor child," said Mrs. Tracy, as she caressed the blind girl. "She ought to go out. I'm going to take her out. It can't be good for her to be shut up in prison all the while. And she must have some new things."

"Prison!" exclaimed Mrs. Cathcart, indignantly. "It isn't any prison at all. She wouldn't be safe if she wasn't locked in. New things? Why, I've thought of that a hundred times. I've a big trunk full of old dresses and things, ready to be made over. There's no need of spending a cent, but I haven't had any time."

"Why, that'll be splendid!" exclaimed Mrs. Tracy, thinking of her friends and their many offers. "We can do all the making over. I do just want to see those things, but I mustn't look at them to-day. If you'll only get them out, ready for us! Why, there's nothing I'd enjoy so much as fixing her up. I always wanted a little girl of my own."

Then they talked of Tom again, and wondered where he was, and all the while he was having the grandest kind of sailing. It was as if Mr. Angus had loaned him the entire use of the Rover for a trip out to sea and around Long Island. Somehow or other, however, when he thought of Mr. Angus, three or four times, he went down to his stateroom and looked under the pillow of the bed, to make sure that his long, white, bunchy envelope of precious papers was safe. "I'm so glad I put it there," he said, "and that it has been kept dry."

Tom thought a great deal about Mr. Angus, and about meeting him in New London, but the money king was not there, any more than he was at sea, as Mr. Gangway imagined. He was all the while in New York city, in the northeasterly corner of it. That is, he was in the country part of the city, that was once part of Westchester county, among farms, and gardens, and villas, where most of the streets and avenues are as yet only laid out on maps. The broad piazza he was sitting in belonged to a very beautiful villa, and he could look out upon Long Island Sound, and see the white sails drift along, and feel entirely retired, and hidden, and restful.

"Rest is what you need, Mr. Angus," said Dr. Harbeck, sitting by him. "But you must get away. What's next?"

"My yacht will be at New London to-morrow, unless she founders at sea," said Mr. Angus. "That is, if Gangway sent my orders to the captain on board, and I'm sure he did. He should have sent my letters and reports here, though."

"I'm glad he didn't," exclaimed the doctor. "They're just what you must not have. Get away from business!"

"Yes, I'll take the morning train for New London, to meet the yacht there," said the rich man, and the doctor went away, leaving behind him a poor fellow whose very life was in danger, just because he was so very rich and knew so well how to make money.

Mr. Angus knew nothing about the excitement at the Australian building. It was by no means over. Mrs. Cruden and her lady friends rested at the head of each flight of stairs, as they went up, but York and Boston did not rest for a moment. They were all yelp and wriggle, as if they had been robbed of something, and wanted to go for it, until at last they got their hungry noses into two saucers of milk. Then the three women sat down, looking very warm, and as if they were also in a state of dreadful suspense.

"For all we know," said Mr. Cruden, "that there safe's been robbed of everything there is in it. It may have been left open a purpose, too."

CHAPTER X.

"Mrs. Cruden," exclaimed Jane, as she recovered her breath a little, "do you mean it? Do you mean that anybody could have left that there safe open, so it could be robbed easy?"

"Such things hev been," said Mrs. Cruden, solemnly, "and everything was clean stole."

Jane and Hannah tried to look at it that way, and in every other way that they could think of, and so did Mrs. Cruden; and they all declared that it seemed as if it were years and years before any news came up stairs.

"Mr. Cruden 'll lose his dinner, and so will Gap," Hannah was saying, when they heard through the open door the sound of approaching footsteps.

One pair came sharply and rapidly, so that Mrs. Cruden exclaimed, "That's Gap! He's the quickest boy 'round here."

The other pair were making long, deliberate strides, as if they belonged to a very tall man.

"Mother," shouted Gap, as he darted in, "there's a hundred thousand dollars gone!"

"Gap!" exclaimed his mother, and Jane and Hannah followed, louder yet; "Gap!" "Gap!"

"Hundred thousand! Gold notes—"

"Gap!" broke in old Mr. Cruden, sternly, solemnly. hoarsely. "Let your mouth be closed. Every tongue present must be closed. It is to be kept secret. If it leaks out, the ends of justice may be defeated. I have done my duty. All men are satisfied with me."

"I'm glad of that," said his wife. "And you won't lose your place. And I'm glad we found the dogs. And Gap was asleep in front of the door all night, and nobody couldn't get in. But I want to know 'bout that hundred thousand dollars right away."

"It's a profound secret," he began again.

"Mother," said Gap, "there didn't anybody get it. It wasn't in the safe."

"How did they steal it, then?" she demanded. "How did it get away? What's become of it? I want to know where it was, if it wasn't in the safe?"

"Why, mother," said Gap, "it wasn't there. They left it lying 'round loose, and they can't tell where it went to. I wish I knew how the pups got down there."

"I don't care about the pups," she said, but her husband drew himself up to his very fullest height, and interrupted her.

"My dear," he said, "stop there. I will relate to you all the circumstances with the utmost punctility."

That was what he went on to do, not omitting the smallest point of the careful manner in which he had swept and regulated Mr. Gangway's office, day after day, or of the reasons why he failed to try the door of the safe on Saturday evening. He grew more and more solemn and stately, as he went on to the experiences of that Sunday morning, the hunt for the lost puppies, the discovery that the safe was open; Gap's hunt for Mr. Gangway, and the final announcement that so many thousands of dollars, "in gold, my dear; solid gold; gold on deposit in the treasury of the United States, is gone! Gone, my dear! And it was not in the safe at all, and nobody can blame me."

"Gone," sighed Mrs. Cruden. "And nobody can tell where!"

That was a dreadful fact to think of, and the afternoon was largely used up in wondering what had been done with all that money, and who had got it. Gap also wondered how York and Boston got down stairs and into the waste basket, but he could hit it pretty nearly. He almost knew, and he said so, that the two black and tans had escaped from their own room when the door was open, had tumbled down the first flight of stairs, had then been picked up by the errand boys of Mr. Gangway's office, and had been made a special deposit of, just as if they had been a kind of money.

Gap failed to guess how the errand boys had hung around Saturday evening, and had had to go home without the puppies after all, just because Mr. Beckwith and Mr. Gangway stayed so much later than usual.

There was plenty of excitement on the land, but Tom Tracy had a very quiet day at sea. All the books and papers on board could not tempt him to read, he had so much to think of. Even after supper, there was nothing else half so pleasant as leaning over the rail and looking at the water, and at the sky, and at the sails of the Rover. He was out of sight of land, away out upon the Atlantic ocean, just as Columbus had been, and Captain Kidd, and Nelson, and Commodore John Paul Jones, and many other distinguished seamen whose names he could remember. He thought a great deal, too, about his mother, and about how she would worry over his unexpected absence, and he wished he could send her word how good a time he was having and not scare her by mentioning the storm. He thought of Amy, and her grandmother, and Crib, and Pete, and the kitten, but he thought even more of the boys he would meet when he got home.

Amy was not thinking of him at all, just then. She had been quiet while Mrs. Tracy was there, and she kept pretty still afterward. Her usual restlessness had all gone away, but some of it seemed to have gone into her grandmother.

"I don't care," exclaimed the old lady just after supper, "I shall have no time to-morrow. I'll just get them out now and look at them."

If Amy knew what was coming she did not say so, but she went and stood by her grandmother during the unlocking of the largest of the trunks which stood against the wall. It was a very large trunk, and it was crammed, packed full of things.

"It hasn't been opened for years and years," muttered Mrs. Cathcart, "but I know what's in it. There's more than she will need, I'm sure of that."

That was plainly true, unless Amy was to have different dresses for every day in the week, twice a day. Out they came, and some of them were silks and satins. Down sat the old woman on the floor, and down sat Amy by her. Neither of them spoke at first, but the blind girl's fingers passed swiftly over the soft surfaces of the fabrics within her reach.

"So soft," she said. "Oh, how pretty they are! Why don't you ever wear them, grandmother?"

"You are to wear them, some of 'em," was all the reply to her question, but Amy had not seen the old lady wipe her eyes, again and again, and now her ears told her what her eyes could not.

"O grandmother!" she exclaimed. "What is the matter! You are crying! Has anybody stolen anything?"

She had thrown her arms around her neck and was hugging and kissing her.

"Not now, Amy. Not just now, they haven't," said Mrs. Cathcart, mournfully. "But if somebody hadn't stolen a great deal, long ago, you wouldn't be here, and I wouldn't be selling peanuts."

"Great Crib!" screamed the parrot from his perch. "Peanuts!"

He added a prolonged screech and some sea phrases, and then he was silent, but Amy remarked, without getting any reply: "Seems to me, grandmother, as if I could think of all sorts of things while I'm touching these dresses. They feel away, 'way back, before I got blind."

She arose and walked away, while the old woman put most of the things back into the trunk, and neither of them spoke for a long time. Not even when it was time to go to bed and sleep.

Amy Cathcart's blind eyes always told her when the lamps were lighted, and she knew when they were put out that night. It made a difference in the kind of darkness.

She did not go to sleep right away, for her mind was busy with a long procession of memories suggested by the touches of her fingers upon the old dresses taken out of her grandmother's trunk. The faces of men and women came to visit her, and she thought she knew them, but she could not call them by their names.

Mr. Rufus Gangway was another person who did not go to sleep quickly, but he was thinking of lost money and of Tom Tracy, and of Mr. Angus. As for the Cruden family, they sat up pretty late, talking about thieves, and Gap took York and Boston to bed with him.

Tom Tracy remained on the deck of the Rover as long as Captain Andrews would let him, watching the waves chase each other, and now and then wishing that he could catch a glimpse of the lighthouse that the mate told him of at Montauk Point. He went to bed in his stateroom at last, and the Rover rocked him to sleep as if she had been a cradle.

It was not easy for any of them, afloat or ashore, to get to bed that night, but it seemed uncommonly easy for all of them to get up early next morning.

TOM AND THE MONEY KING.		179

Tom Tracy had an early breakfast, and a good one, and he did not know how near his mother came to cooking something extra good to put on his plate. When he got on deck he looked around eagerly for Montauk Point, and was just going to ask about it when the captain touched his elbow.

"There, Tom," he said, "there's Block Island, and away off yonder is Point Judith. We're running fine! We'll get to New London in no time."

The Rover was, indeed, dancing along splendidly, and Tom felt it, all over, as he stood and looked and looked until the mate came and said: "We've got there, my boy. We're running in now. Can't you see the fort, away yonder? And the shore batteries? That's where the fight was, in the old Revolutionary War, when Arnold, the traitor, came and burned New London."

Tom was ready enough to hear about the fights and the massacre at Fort Griswold; and then the mate left him, and the Rover swept on into the harbor, taking in sail as she went. While she was doing so, a man upon one of the wharves was watching her. He took a white handkerchief from his pocket and swung it, and it seemed to have

a controlling influence over the yacht, for
she steered at once for that wharf, and ran
in gracefully alongside of it.

Tom had been below after his precious
envelope, and when he came on deck there sat
Mr. Angus, listening to Captain Andrews'

MR. ANGUS, LISTENING TO CAPTAIN ANDREWS' REPORT.

report of the good behavior of the Rover
during the storm.

"I'm glad she's all right," said the money
king, glancing over her from stem to stern,
but his eyes came down from a search of
her spars and rigging, to look into the eager,
boyish face of the one passenger.

"Now, Tom," he said.

"Mr. Gangway sent me, sir," said Tom, as he delivered the envelope, but he could not think what else to say.

"Tom," said Mr. Angus, with a grim smile, as he took the envelope, "you look as if you had been through a storm at sea."

"I guess I have," said Tom, coloring; "and I've had a ride for nothing."

"I don't know about that," laughed Mr. Angus. "I may make you pay for the use of my yacht. Salt water isn't good for straw hats, though."

Tom's hat had stuck to his head wonderfully while he was under water, but it had afterward dried with independent twists, before and behind. His clothes, too, had dried, but his trowsers were an inch and a half shorter and a size tighter than before, and so was his coat. He had now no collar on nor necktie, and his shoes were anything but shining.

"Hello! what's this?" was the sudden exclamation he next heard from Mr. Angus. "What on earth did Gangway send them for! Is the man crazy?"

He had opened the envelope, and some letters came out first and some folded papers,

but these were followed by a thin packet,
just such as can be made with a rubber band
around ten thin slips of tough paper, each
a little larger than a banknote. They had
a clear, yellow tint to look at, and so they
were not greenbacks, but Mr. Angus counted
them and remarked: "One hundred thousand dollars! It's a mistake. It's a blunder. I must send them back to Rufus Gangway. Tom, come below with me."

Tom followed him down into the cabin,
thinking fast about the yellow papers and
about the figure he was cutting.

"Mr. Gangway told me," he said, "not to
deliver it to anybody but you."

"That's right, Tom," said Mr. Angus,
"but did you see Mr. Gangway put these
gold notes into this envelope?"

"He didn't put 'em in," said Tom. "The
envelope lay on his table. I saw him take
it up and put in the other things, and seal
it, and hand it to me. They must have been
in it when he picked it up."

"Then Rufe's in a peck of trouble about
them now," said Mr. Angus. "Serve him
right, too, for getting excited. But you're
the boy I want this morning. Wait."

He opened a writing-desk that stood in the cabin, and he sat down and wrote rapidly for a few minutes.

"There, Tom Tracy," he said, as he ceased writing. "I wish that you knew a little more than you do. Take that to Dr. Harbeck, and see him first. Take that to Mr. Gangway. Take the others to their addresses. But I can't afford to have my errands done by a scarecrow."

"I guess I do look kind o' washed out," said Tom, squirming and coloring.

"Your rigging has suffered badly," said Mr. Angus. "I owe you a new outfit. Now, you obey my orders. When you get to the city, rig up before you see one of those men. Buy just what I tell you, and it's none of your business why, or what it costs."

He gave close directions, which could only be filled in a firstclass clothing store, and he even named the place, telling Tom that when he should come out of it he would be a different looking boy — or, as he said, "bird."

He handed Tom a hundred dollars, and added: "Keep an account, and settle with me when I see you. You've just time to catch the train. Go!"

Tom picked up his warped hat and went on deck. The captain, and the mate, and the sailors shouted good-bye to him as he hurried ashore, and then he hurried off toward the railway depot.

It was just as Mr. Angus said, for he barely succeeded in catching the train that was ready. All the way to the depot, however, and while buying his ticket, and after getting into a car, he felt worse and worse about the wreck of his clothing.

"Scarecrow!" he said to himself. "Well, I guess that's just about how I look."

He forgot it, now and then, as the swift express carried him to the city, but he remembered it, awfully, after he walked into the great clothing store, and spoke to a nobby clerk.

"Clothing, sir? Ah, — well, — yes, — certainly," began the clerk, but Tom was thinking.

"It doesn't seem right, somehow, but I've got to obey orders! It's awful, but I've got to get the best there is!"

That was how he came to astonish the clerk, for he put away suit after suit, insist-

ing upon looking at "something better'n
that, I guess."

Tom felt a queer feeling that a yachtsman
or any other great sailor ought to wear
dark, navy blue, and that was what he
picked out. It was a very stylish suit, and
before he put it on, he bought new under-
clothing, throughout, with a new necktie,
shirt, collar, cuffs, hat, and shoes. Then he
went into the dressing-room the salesman
led him to, and put on everything, making
a bundle of his shipwrecked rigging. The
pleasure and excitement of it grew as he
went along, and he had never felt so well in
his life as he did when it was finished, and
he took a look at himself in a full-length
mirror.

"Not much of a scarecrow, now," he was
saying to himself. "I guess I'll take one of
those nickel-headed canes. This is just what
Mr. Angus told me to do."

But just then the salesman came up, with
a very polite bow.

"Here's your change, sir. Your bill was
fifty dollars and seventy-five cents. Hope
you'll like it, sir, and call again."

Tom had expected the change, but he took
the something else that was handed him

with a start of astonishment. It was a
very neat American watch and chain, of a
metal closely resembling gold.

"Every customer for over fifty dollars,"
explained the salesman, "before August
tenth, gets one of 'em. Good time-pieces.
Nine men out of ten can't say but what
they're gold."

"Advertising dodge," exclaimed Tom.
"I'll just put it on. Then I'll get me a
cane."

So he did, and when he got out upon
Broadway with his cane in his hand, it
seemed to him as if the people he met were
all disposed to admire his blue suit. He had
his errands all before him, however, and he
turned them over in his mind, as he walked
along.

"What'll mother say," he said to himself,
"when she sees me? And father? And Mr.
Gangway? Amy can't see me, and she
won't know the difference. I just don't
want to meet any of the boys. Now for
Mr. Harbeck's first, and won't I astonish
him!"

That might be, but then Tom Tracy did
not exactly know the doctor.

CHAPTER XI.

TOM had an idea that his new clothes not only made him well dressed, but that they gave him the air of a man of business. He felt that he had very important business upon his hands, and he walked fast. Perhaps he learned something more about how he looked after he reached Dr. Harbeck's office, and stood, for a moment, with the gray eyes of the great physician searching him all over for symptoms of what he had been doing with his money.

"Has it all gone?" asked the doctor, drily. "Why didn't you follow my prescription?"

"I did," said Tom, blushing to his eyes. "All that money is locked up. I haven't spent a cent of it. But, doctor, that letter's from Mr. Angus, at New London. I left him on board the Rover."

The letter which Tom handed to the doctor seemed to come open in his hand as he took it, but he read it thoughtfully, and as he finished he remarked: "I'm glad he is feeling better. He'll be all right if he takes care of himself. Now, Tom, go ahead. Tell me everything."

Tom was eager to do that. He told all about the cruise of the Rover to begin with, and he received quite a number of appreciative nods from the doctor as he went along, but when he had finished all that and had explained the mystery of the new suit of clothes he suddenly struck into an altogether different subject.

"Doctor," he said, "do you know how to cure a blind girl? If you do, I'll give you back that hundred dollars for curing her."

There came into the doctor's face a sudden flush and flash of interest.

"Blind girl?" he said. "Tell me all you know about her."

Tom tried hard to do so, and the doctor helped him with a curious lot of questions. Her fondness for music, and how she played the piano, and how she wanted to hear more, and how she remembered old days, and how she walked around her room. Tom told it all, and then Dr. Harbeck almost shut his eyes while he remarked:

"She notes a difference between day and night. Music. Light. Not total blindness. Tom, I do n't believe I can cure that girl, but I'll try. I must see her, but I do n't want her to know I see her or what I see

"BLIND GIRL? TELL ME ALL YOU KNOW ABOUT HER."

her for. I won't come to her house. Next week, Thursday evening, there's to be a concert of instrumental and vocal music at the Grand opera house. I'll send you tickets. Bring her there. There will be a glare of light. I will tell you then what I want you to do next. Go along, now."

Tom went out of the house with a beating
at his heart, for he had done much more
than he had expected to do, and it had
stirred him up so that he had forgotten all
about his new suit or how he looked in it.

"Now for the other errands," he said to
himself, aloud, and on he went down town.
He was just going into the Australian building when he heard a voice behind him:
"Just got back from Chiny? O, but, isn't
he a swell! Oh, my!"

"I can't stop now, Gap," said Tom. "I'll
see you by and by."

"Why didn't you get a fan and an
umbrella?" shouted Gap, but Tom was
hurrying in, and in a moment more he was
at Mr. Gangway's desk.

"This way, Tom. Don't speak," said the
speculator, as he arose and led the way into
a corner of the room.

"That's from him," said Tom, delivering
the letter from Mr. Angus.

"Don't say a word. Don't mention his
name," said Mr. Gangway, as he tore open
the envelope.

He read the letter quickly enough, and
then, with a very red face, he counted ten

slips of gold yellow paper which he found in
the same envelope.

"That's where they were, is it?" he muttered. "I must have put them there myself.
I don't see how I could have done it and
not have known it, but here they are. Beckwith is all right and so is old Cruden. Tom,
this thing is all explained. Don't say anything. Don't answer anybody's questions.
Come here to-morrow morning. Remember
that you don't know where Mr. Angus is,
nor where you've been, nor what you've
been doing.

"All right, Mr. Gangway," said Tom, and
out he went, feeling a little older and larger
for having so much secret to keep.

He had other errands to do before he could
go home, but he was getting very eager to
see his mother. For her part, Tom had
seemed to her a kind of lost boy ever since
Saturday evening. Never before had he
been away from her so long, and now she
could not even guess where he might be.
Somehow or other, however, the more she
thought of him the more earnest she became
in her purposes concerning Amy Cathcart.

"Grandmother?" she said to herself.

"Humph! What that poor child needs is a mother! I'll go right to see her."

When she went for the key, she found the peanut business too brisk for any long talk with Mrs. Cathcart, and she really did not care to have any.

"Amy!" she thought, as she took the key and walked on. "There, all alone, in prison all day. Poor child! I wish she belonged to me. I'm going to see her, anyhow."

It was very much as if Amy had been waiting for somebody to come. When Mrs. Tracy got there and unlocked the door and opened it, there stood the blind girl holding out her hands.

"It isn't Tom," she said, "I know his step on the stairs. It's you—"

"Tom's away," said Mrs. Tracy. "He didn't get home. I've come to take you with me, to stay all day. I've seen your grandmother."

Amy found herself swept into a great, motherly hug, so tightly that all she had breath to say was, "Where has Tom gone?"

"He's a lubber!" screamed Crib. "Port! Port! Peanuts! Hurrah!"

Mrs. Tracy told all there was to tell, while she was packing a large basket with selections from the things which Mrs. Cathcart had left out for her. All the while there was a stream of noisy criticisms from Crib, but at last all was ready, including Amy, and she and Mrs. Tracy were on their way to the Probus building.

It was all like a dream to the blind girl, and Mrs. Tracy herself said that, what between her and the big basket, it was about the most remarkable walk she had ever taken. Amy clung pretty closely to her in the street, and could hardly be made to answer yes or no, but that was nothing to the way in which she held her breath and hugged Mrs. Tracy's arm while they were going up in the elevator.

The women Mrs. Tracy had spoken to on Sunday must have talked about it afterward, for there were several of them at dinner that day, in the ninth story of the Probus building. One of them, more thoughtful upon that point, because she had been a milliner, had brought along a pair of hats which could be trimmed over, she said, and made every bit as good as new.

It was almost a terrible kind of time for poor Amy. She was measured and measured, and the stuffs the old dresses were
13

made of were turned over and over, and
were discussed and criticised, ever so long,
until at last there suddenly came a sound
as of the quick ripping of a seam, and actual
work had begun. The whole party of vol-
unteers, dressmakers and milliners, were
entirely absorbed in this work, when Amy
suddenly stood erect and listened, as if she
had heard something which they had not,
and in another moment the door opened.

"Tom!" screamed Mrs. Tracy. "O Tom,
where have you been?"

She had no chance to say another word
at once, for Tom was in as great a hurry to
kiss his mother as she was to kiss him.
Then she held him out at arm's length to
look at him, and again she asked: "Where
have you been? What does this mean?"

"I've been at sea, mother," he whispered,
with a quick glance around him, and she
was just whispering back: "Oh! I understand! Business," when Amy touched his
arm.

"It's new," she said. "It's another coat.
How nice it feels!"

"Yes, Amy," he replied, "it's all new, but
I must go, now."

"O Tom," she exclaimed, "I'm so glad you got back safe! Your mother was so afraid—"

"I'm all right," said Tom. "I'm coming to see you pretty soon. Mother, I've got to hurry off. I'll come back."

And out he dashed, for a rain of inquiries had begun. Every one of those women knew him, and they had all been astonished at his new clothes, his watch and chain, and his cane. So had his mother, wisely as she had held her tongue, and so was his father when Tom met him in one of the corridors of the Probus building.

"I just want to see you, father," began Tom.

"Who paid for those things, Tom," said Mr. Tracy, eyeing his son from head to foot. "You didn't?"

"No, I guess not," said Tom; "but I've got to tell you a good deal this time."

"Go ahead, Tom," said his father, "but look out what you say."

He put his thumbs into the armholes of his vest and looked at his son with a glow of pride and exultation on his face, while Tom told about the voyage of the Rover. He got as far as his meeting Mr. Angus, but there the prim janitor suddenly stopped him.

"Hold on, Tom!" he exclaimed. "I don't want to know his business. It isn't mine to know. Don't tell."

"GO AHEAD, TOM, BUT LOOK OUT WHAT YOU SAY."

"That's a fact," said Tom, "and Mr. Gangway cautioned me—"

"Shut right up, Tom," said his father. "I'm bringing you up. A boy that can't be trusted not to know anything isn't worth a cent."

Tom fully agreed with him, but he had to hear more about the nice point of honor his father was trying to teach him, so that he might grow up fit to be trusted with keys and offices and important doors and safes. At the end of it Tom felt almost as proud as did his father, over the confidence already reposed in him, and he walked off to see what he could do with himself until tea time.

It was well for the women in his mother's parlor that they had something to busy them, so sure were they all that there was a secret of some kind connected with Tom Tracy's absence, and his sudden return, and his wonderfully fine clothes. They may even have worked harder over Amy's hats and dresses, but they were worried about it, until finally Tom himself came in again and all work stopped at once. That was not the worst of it, for he now felt at liberty to tell them that he had been out at sea in a yacht. He told about the storm, too, and his mother came and put her arm around him, and Amy came and sat down by him, and all the visitors put away their sewing and departed, one by one, painfully sure that Tom had had twice as much more to tell, if he would only have told it.

"Tom," said his mother, "you can take Amy home. She's got to get supper ready for her grandmother. She's going to be dressed real nicely, and she's got a new hat ready to wear home."

That brought out something about the concert, but not a word of Dr. Harbeck that Amy was permitted to hear. That part of it was explained to Mrs. Tracy in a whisper, in the kitchen, and it seemed to excite her even more than the story of the storm, for the storm was over, and Tom was safe, but Dr. Harbeck and the concert were yet to come.

If Tom had been aware that he was well dressed, ever since he put on his new suit, he knew it twice as well while he was walking home with Amy, but all she seemed to know anything about was the danger he had been in, and, after that, the wonderful idea of the concert.

Gap Cruden went to bed half an hour earlier than usual that evening. He had almost seemed to lose his interest in York and Boston. It was all because of Tom Tracy's blue suit and watch and chain, and Gap went to sleep thinking how nice it would be to have a watch ticking, or to wake up in the morning and see it hanging there and know at once if it were time to get up.

Tom Tracy himself looked at his watch a number of times in the course of the evening, and his mother admired it exceedingly, but his father was even more interested in making him write out an account of the way he had spent Mr. Angus' money.

Amy Cathcart's evening was in a sort of new world, and there was a notable change even in her grandmother. The old lady examined the new hat again and again, and between each look and the next she had a time of sitting down and thinking, while Crib screeched his extreme dislike of that bit of millinery.

Perhaps there was less anxiety in several places that night to keep people awake, but the next morning came as usual. Precisely at ten o'clock, as ordered, Tom Tracy walked into Mr. Gangway's office, and he found that gentleman sitting alone.

"Tom," said Mr. Gangway, "where were you brought up?"

"Right here," said Tom. "My father's janitor of the Probus building."

"I see, I see," said Mr. Gangway. "You went to this kind of school. Here's where you learned how to keep your eyes open and your mouth shut."

"Father says a boy that can't, isn't worth a cent," replied Tom.

"He's right," said Mr. Gangway. "Now, I'll pay you for this trip."

"I guess not," said Tom. "I've been paid once. Mr. Angus made me dress up, and he paid for it, and I've some of his money left. You ought not to pay me while he does."

"Right again," said Mr. Gangway. "Now you've to make another trip, and this, too, is for him. That is, it's for him and me both. Buy one of those alligator-leather gripsacks to carry your things in."

"Yes, sir, I will," said Tom, and then he shut his mouth hard, so as not to let out one of a lot of questions that were tumbling around in it, trying very hard to speak.

"I'll have everything ready for you at five o'clock," said Mr. Gangway, just as if he supposed Tom had already been told a great deal by Mr. Angus. "You are to take the night train for Boston, and be waiting on the wharf when the Rover runs in. Mr. Angus doesn't mean to come ashore there or to see anybody. Have a boat ready to put you on board. Buy all the Boston morning papers to take to him, and any others you can get."

"I understand," said Tom, trying desperately to appear cool and easy.

"Come here at five," said Mr. Gangway. "Say nothing to anybody."

Tom's head did not seem to him to be clear, after that, until he found himself carrying a neat, alligator-leather traveling bag that he had bought. His first errand was to find his father.

"Father," he said, when they met, "I'm off again. It's another long errand."

"Stop right there," said Mr. Tracy. "Remember what I've taught you. I hope it'll be a good trip. Go and tell your mother. Learn all you can while you're gone. Show 'em that you're to be trusted. Honor bright!"

He looked proud enough, just then, but Tom felt at liberty to say:

"It's to Boston and back, father."

"Go ahead, Tom," said Mr. Tracy.

"That's all I want to know. I can trust you myself! Ahem."

He turned right away, then, walking very straight, and Tom went to see his mother with a strong feeling growing within him that of all things in the world it was the best and proudest to feel that he could be trusted.

Mrs. Tracy was hardly as well pleased at first as her husband had been, but she became better and better reconciled to her son's new errand the more she talked about it, and then she had a great deal to tell him about Boston.

"I'm going to Amy's this afternoon," she said, "to try on her first new dress. I'll tell her why you don't come."

"Mother," said Tom, "when you go, I'll go along. I won't stay but a minute."

"You can go," said Mrs. Tracy, "and you can carry my bundles. There's another hat almost done, and a white dress that's going to be nice enough for her to wear at the concert."

"Won't that be splendid!" said Tom.

Dinner-time came, and, not long afterward, Tom and his mother, with her friend Miss Higbee, who had made the new hats,

were standing by Mrs. Cathcart's peanut-
stand, asking for the key. A gentleman,
who was passing by, stopped suddenly and
beckoned Tom.

"You remember me?" he asked.

"Guess I do," said Tom. "You're Judge
Carpenter, Mr. Angus' lawyer."

"And you are Tom Tracy," said the
judge. "Isn't that your mother? What
name did you call the woman that keeps the
peanut-stand?"

"That's my mother," said Tom. "The
old lady is Mrs. Cathcart."

"Where does she live?" asked the sharp-
faced lawyer. "Do you know anything
about her?"

"Corner of Garnet and Burgoyne streets,"
said Tom. "She was born there."

Just then he saw on Judge Carpenter's
face a strange expression of triumph.

"Found them, have I?" he exclaimed.
"Mr. Angus ought to know at once. I wish
I could see him, or send word to him, but
he's out at sea. Away out—"

"If it's anything he ought to know," said
Tom, "I can take it right to him."

"Hurrah!" exclaimed the lawyer, with a
quick, chopped-off laugh. "Oh, my soul!

Three cheers! Now, Tom, are you going right off?"

"To-night," said Tom.

"Come to my office, then, before you go," said the lawyer. "I'll have some papers ready. I sha'n't ask you where he is. In fact, I've really got to be able to say that I don't know."

"I wouldn't tell you," said Tom. "But I'll come for the papers. Mother's calling me—"

"Of course you wouldn't tell," he heard the lawyer say, "unless you wanted to lose your place; but if this isn't going to be a big piece of business!"

CHAPTER XII.

A LONG ERRAND FOR TOM.

Mrs. Cathcart had not seemed inclined to say much about either millinery or dressmaking to her granddaughter's lady friends, but she had given them the key. As soon as Tom finished his talk with Judge Carpenter and came back to them, therefore, they were ready to go on with their errand.

Miss Higbee was every inch as much excited about it as was either Tom or his mother, and they all walked pretty rapidly. When they reached what Mrs. Tracy called "Amy's prison" and opened it, Amy, too, appeared to be excited. Perhaps, too, she was awed by the presence of Miss Higbee, and she had very little to say while Tom was there, but Crib made up for it. Tom was talking with him when his mother came and told him it was time for him to go.

If Tom had wondered why a gentleman like Judge Carpenter should ask questions about a poor old woman like Mrs. Cathcart, she herself was even astonished at the way in which the lawyer bought goods of her. He knew her name, too, and he knew where she lived, and that she was born there, and he talked all the time.

"Oranges? Yes," he said. "Half a dozen. Pint of peanuts. They're charging too much rent for rooms in those old houses. Half a dozen bananas—"

"I don't pay any rent, and I won't," she said. "I've a perfect right to live there. My granddaughter's title to that place is as good as anybody's. I guess nobody owns it, if we don't. I won't pay a cent."

"Give me another pint of peanuts," said the lawyer. "I wouldn't pay a cent, if I were you. Every soul of 'em ought to pay you, instead of you paying them. I know how it is. I know all about it, Mrs. Cathcart. You're an injured woman."

"That's what I am," she said, "and I'm glad you know—" and then she went on and he went on, and everything she told him he told her back again, with more added to it, and when at last he walked away, his coat-tail pockets were sticking out with fruit and peanuts and confectionery. He said to himself: "It's the best day's work I've done in a long time. It'll be a good thing for her, too, and for her granddaughter. Blind, eh? Sorry for that. Now I must see Tom Tracy and get all he knows."

"IT'S THE BEST DAY'S WORK I'VE DONE IN A LONG TIME."

Whether or not to tell anything at all about the Cathcarts was already a puzzle in Tom's mind, and it was not rooted out in a brief talk he had with Judge Carpenter, when he got to that gentleman's office. He was surprised at how much the lawyer already knew, as well as at the size of the package of papers he gave him to put into

his gripsack. There was little room for
more in that bag after Mrs. Tracy had put
in the shirts, collars, and things she deemed
needful for a trip to Boston, and the sandwiches and other provisions she believed he
would eat on the way.

A little before five o'clock he almost
startled her.

"Mother," he said, suddenly, "now for
Mr. Gangway's errand. I'm off!"

It was hard to let him go, but he went.

That Tuesday was a peculiar day for Gap
Cruden, for he woke up thinking of Tom
Tracy's new suit and watch and chain, and
of how to get something like them for himself. York and Boston danced and yelped
about him in vain, for he gave them nothing
but their breakfast, and they had never
before seen Gap do so much brushing. His
hair, clothes, shoes, got it in turn, and he
tied his necktie three times. He did his
morning errands promptly, and he was in
the office of Strong & Bullard earlier than
even the bookkeeper. All day long he dashed
around like the best office-boy in New York,
and he felt pretty sure of a brilliant future
until about three o'clock. At that hour he
saw another boy, of about his age or older,

coming out of old Mr. Strong's private room, and in a moment more he was himself called in for a short talk with the head of the firm. It was a conversation which ended with:

"Well, Cruden, you can refer to me. You have your faults, but you are a good boy. Eat too many peanuts; don't get back as quick as you might; talk too much; leave orange peels on the floor. Well, well, I'll give you a good character. Good-bye, Gap."

"I don't want to go home and tell father," groaned Gap, as he slowly walked out of the office, after the bookkeeper had paid him a week's wages. "Old Strong is wrong about the orange peel. Some of the customers did that. "I don't think I eat too many peanuts, but I'll break off. Anyhow, I'll watch the shucks."

It seemed a gloomy day, in spite of the bright July sunshine, and all that part of the city seemed gloomy to Gap, as he walked around in it, but at last he found himself in front of the Australian building, almost without intending it.

"Hello, Gap," he heard behind him. "What's the matter?"

14

"Tom," said Gap, "I wish I was going to China."

Tom understood that something awful had happened, and his next questions were so full of boyish sympathy that Gap told him just how it was.

"You're always kind o' lucky," said Gap, "but I kind o' slip up. Don't you know of a place? There's more boys!"

Tom knew that. Twenty boys for every good place. He felt badly for Gap.

"You pitch in and hunt for one," he said, "and I'll speak to father. He knows everybody. I won't be gone but a day or two."

"It's the worst kind of luck," said Gap.

"I've got to go," and Gap saw Tom dash into the building.

"That's the way he always does," said Gap.

Mr. Gangway was sitting behind his desk when Tom came in.

"All ready," he said in a low voice. "There, put that into your sack. Don't let it go out of your hand. Get right out. I wish I had an errand boy. We've had to discharge those two monkeys."

"Gap Cruden," said Tom. "His father's

janitor of this building. He's outside, now. Shall I send him in?''

"Send him right in," said Mr. Gangway. "I'll find out about him."

Tom and his sack were out where Gap could see them again with a quickness that astonished him, and so did the news Tom brought.

"Tom," said Gap, "I'll go right in. Where are you going? I won't tell."

"Gap," said Tom, "if Mr. Gangway heard you ask a fool question like that you wouldn't stay in his office ten minutes. It's a place where nobody knows anything."

"That's it," thought Gap, as he walked in. "Did I ever ask too many questions? I'll never ask any more."

He did not feel like asking any when he looked into the iron face of Mr. Rufus Gangway, and he did not have many to answer. He was simply given an errand to do, away up town, and was told to report at eight o'clock next morning. He came within a breath of asking what he was to do next, but a flash of wisdom hit him in time, and he was off at once.

" He might do," said Mr. Gangway. "Why, he didn't even look around the room. It

can't be that there are two boys like Tom
Tracy. Well, no; on the whole, I guess not.
Tom's been trained to it. That boy'll
amount to something if he keeps on. He
can shut his mouth like an oyster."

Tom himself had yet another thought
upon his mind, and it carried him, next, into
Dr. Harbeck's office.

"Just what I was wishing for," said the
doctor, as he wrote on a slip of paper, after
Tom had told his errand. Then he put up
some powders and two small bottles, and
made a packet of them for Tom to take
with him.

"See me at once when you return," said
the doctor. "I've ordered tickets for the
concert. I'm interested in that case."

"I'm glad of that," said Tom. "Now, I
mustn't miss the express train."

He did not. He even had time to spare;
but Gap Cruden missed his supper, and he
was a hungry boy when he reached home,
after his first errand for Mr. Gangway. He
had something worse than hunger on his
mind, too, and he did not go at once for a
look at York and Boston. He even stood
still and said nothing, while old Mr. Cruden
stood and looked at him.

"Where have you been, Gap?" he asked. "What has made you so late?"

"I ain't at Strong & Bullard's any more," blurted out Gap. "I'm with Mr. Gangway."

"You don't say!" exclaimed his mother.

Then Gap had to sit still until she and his father and Hannah and Jane had asked him all the questions and said all the things that belonged to his losing one place and getting another. Before they were done, however, Mrs. Cruden had a pretty good supper ready for Gap.

"He may eat this time," said Mr. Cruden, sternly. "I did say he shouldn't, but he may. He's got to be more punctil. I'll do my duty by him; so will Mr. Gangway. He's got his place on my account. It's because I guarded that safe—"

"And saved him that hundred thousand dollars," said Mrs. Cruden, triumphantly, for they had heard of its recovery that day.

"I felt sure," said Hannah, "that something would come out of that for Gap."

"So did I," said Jane, but neither she nor any of the others explained why.

Tom Tracy slept pretty well that night in a berth in a railway sleeping-car, hugging his precious alligator-leather bag, but he was awakened before daylight by the conductor, with a shoulder-shake and the word, "Boston!"

"Boston?" replied Tom, and he was up and ready when the train rolled into the railway depot.

He walked out of that very wide awake, but under a curious impression that anybody entering Boston would see the Bunker Hill monument and Faneuil Hall right away.

It was yet too dark to see anything very clearly, and all he could do was to go to a hotel and wait until breakfast-time. Even before he ate anything, however, he surprised the man who kept the hotel newsstand. It was not often that one boy bought all the morning papers and a lot of other newspapers, and not one story paper.

"I guess Mr. Angus doesn't want any stories," thought Tom, "but I'll take him everything else."

That was probably correct, but his first thought after breakfast had an error in it.

"I guess a fellow that can find his way around New York can find his way around

Boston," he remarked, as he got into what he supposed to be the right street car. "Now for the harbor!"

That was his error, and he tried six different car lines, and walked, and asked any number of questions, and got tired and hot and anxious before he saw anything that looked like a harbor.

At last he went down a street, at the end of which, through a kind of narrow twist in the buildings, he saw a patch of water.

"That's it," he shouted, "I was almost beginning to think there wasn't any."

A very long pier reached out into the water, and Tom's breath came and went faster as he walked out to the end of it, for it was now nearly ten o'clock, and he began to feel as if he were getting to business behind time. Ships, steamers, lighters, tug-boats along the wharves, coming, going, business driving, bustle, work in all directions—how should he hope to find the Rover?

He stood at the very end of the pier, looking seaward, and the more he looked the more despairing he felt.

"She might be anywhere," he said, "miles and miles away, just as if she were somewhere around New York, and I did n't know where."

He had hardly calculated that if he was looking for the Rover, she might also be looking for him. He had just noticed a rowboat with a man in it, close at hand, when he was startled all over.

TOM GOING OUT TO THE ROVER.

"There she is!" he shouted. "Hello, boat! Mister! I'll give you a dollar to put me aboard of that yacht."

There she was, slipping along slowly, gracefully, and a man on deck was looking along the shore with a glass.

"You do n't say!" he exclaimed. "Mr. Angus, here comes Tom Tracy."

Tom was coming, and the hardest work he ever did was to keep cool and look cool when he shook hands with the captain on the deck of the Rover.

"We've had a splendid run," said the captain. "Mr. Angus has gone below. Go right along down."

Tom went, and by a table in the cabin sat the man of too much money.

"How d'ye do, Tom?" he said. "Sit down. Show me what you've got. I'm listening."

Tom began to open his bag, and at the same time to tell his story.

"Don't leave out anything," said Mr. Angus, as he opened the envelopes, and then he pulled a bell-cord, and down came Captain Andrews.

"Put to sea," said Mr. Angus. "It'll take me all day to clear up these things. Now I've got the newspapers, we needn't send ashore. Get out of the harbor as quick as you can. Go ahead, Tom." So Tom went ahead with his story, and all the while the Rover was flitting away seaward.

It was about two hours before Tom boarded her that Gap Cruden, in New York, again entered the office of Mr. Rufus Gangway. The one clerk already there nodded to him, but said nothing. When Mr. Beckwith, the bookkeeper, came in, he, too, nodded and said nothing, but opened the

safe, took out books and papers, and went
to work. If it had been at Strong &
Bullard's, Gap would surely have said something. He might even have been eating
peanuts to pass away the time. He did
catch himself wishing that he had York and
Boston for company, but just then Mr.
Beckwith set him to copying letters, and he
felt proud enough that he knew how to
work a copy-press. Even while doing it,
however, he had to bite his tongue to keep
it from telling Mr. Beckwith how he had
done his errand of the previous evening, and
again to keep from asking when Mr. Gangway would come in.

"Tom Tracy wouldn't peep," said Gap to
himself, and he kept still.

Mr. Gangway came at last, and Gap over-
heard a little of what Mr. Beckwith said to
him, at his desk.

"Was he on time?" asked Mr. Gangway.

"Here when I came," said Mr. Beckwith.
"Takes right hold. Hasn't said a word.
Mighty spry."

"Perhaps he'll do. Gap!"

If ever Gap tried to put a story into few
words, it was in telling his errand then.

"That 'll do," said Mr. Gangway. "How much did Strong & Bullard give you?"

"Five dollars a week," said Gap.

"Six, then, here," said Mr. Gangway, "but look sharp. No nonsense about this office. Mr. Beckwith wants you."

Gap turned to the bookkeeper, and all he knew of errand-running had to be called up, in order to obey that man's rapid instructions. It was very hard not to ask how he was to do this thing, and where he was to find that man, and if that firm had not moved, but Gap set his teeth and got away in silence. His first errand carried him past Mrs. Cathcart's peanut-stand, and he was an old customer of hers. He could smell some freshly roasted peanuts, but he went right by them without stopping. They had been too much temptation for a tall gentleman with a very sharp face. He was buying a whole quart at once. Gap did not know who he was, but Mrs. Cathcart seemed to know him.

"Some of the biggest men on Wall street eat peanuts," said Gap, to himself, with an injured air.

"No, Mr. Carpenter," Mrs. Cathcart said, just then, "there isn't any doubt about it.

I can show you all the papers. Amy's the only living soul belonging to that family, and her grandfather owned it all. I can prove it."

"So can I, Mrs. Cathcart," said Mr. Carpenter. "I'll come, some evening, and show you my papers, if you'd like to see them. It occurred to me that you might like to look at them. I've some that were signed by your husband."

"I don't half believe he did," she said. "Just you bring them and let me see them. No living soul besides myself knows what you've been telling me, and I'd like to know how you ever came to know it. You come and let me see those papers. I'll show you some you never saw."

He finished his talk with her and walked slowly away, eating peanuts and throwing the shucks on the sidewalk as if he had been an office-boy out of a place, but he was saying to himself: "That's about all Angus needs. If we can get hold of that property, through her and her granddaughter, we can buy off everybody else, and we can put a building on it as big as a fort!"

CHAPTER XIII.

THE BLIND GIRL AND THE MUSIC.

AT the very hour when Judge Carpenter was making such extraordinary remarks about Mrs. Cathcart and her granddaughter and the house they lived in, Mr. Angus, down in the cabin of the Rover, was busily looking over the different lots of papers which Tom Tracy had brought him. Oddly enough, the money king also was thinking of the old peanut woman and of the blind girl and of the rickety, dingy, worn-out old buildings at the corner of Garnet and Burgoyne streets. He finished all the papers, at last, and put them aside, and opened the little parcel sent by Dr. Harbeck.

"Tom," he said, as he uncorked a bottle of medicine, "who told you to see him?"

"You did, sir," replied Tom. "You sent me there. Of course, I went for his answer."

"You're right!" said Mr. Angus. "I like

that. I guess you can do an errand. Now for Rufe Gangway's reports."

Tom sat still while the money king read them, and while he penciled figures on a piece of paper.

"I think I won't read the news now," said Mr. Angus, at last. "I must see the captain, though. Come along, Tom."

They went up on deck, and Tom was beginning to feel vastly better acquainted with his somewhat grim and silent employer, into whose services he had drifted, he hardly knew how. Mr. Angus chatted for a minute with the captain, and then he left Tom to play passenger once more, while he himself went down into the cabin again to disobey Dr. Harbeck by plunging into business at his desk in the cabin.

Tom Tracy had not been kidnapped this time, and there was no prospect of a storm to interfere with the splendid sail he was having. He felt better, too, about his mother and the state of her mind during his absence. He had an astonishment at the dinner table, however. Not that it was so fine a dinner, but that Mr. Angus talked to him about Amy, and her blindness, and her grandmother, and the house they lived

in, and the way they lived, and seemed to
take a deep interest in them. He even said
he would write to Dr. Harbeck about Amy,
and added: "We'll put you ashore to-morrow, Tom, and you need n't miss the concert. I can guess why Harbeck wants her
to go."

That was more than Tom could do; but
after a grand day at sea he slept when night
came in the same stateroom he had been
pitched around in by the storm. When
morning came, and he went up for another
look at the ocean, the sun was just rising,
brilliantly. The view eastward was magnificent, but when Tom turned and looked
toward the west he felt a thrill all over him.

"That's North America," he exclaimed.
"That's the way it looked to Columbus!"

"I guess he never saw that coast," said
Captain Andrews, near him, "and we won't
see it any closer to-day unless the wind
changes. We're trying to beat in so we can
put you ashore."

Tom could hardly feel badly over the prospect of another day at sea, and he said so,
but the change of wind came at last, and
the captain and Mr. Angus had their way,
but not so early as they had wished.

There were signs all that day that Mrs. Tracy was getting a dislike for Boston, and that she doubted Tom's safety in that place. When evening came she had more to say about it, and Mr. Tracy had to argue with her. Still, he did not urge her to go to bed, and he was lying asleep on the sofa as late as ten o'clock, and she sat by the table sewing, and stopping to listen.

"My dear!" she exclaimed, suddenly, "that's the doorbell! Tom's come home!"

It rang three times before Mr. Tracy could get away down stairs and raise the shutters, but even then Tom was not permitted to report the whole of his Boston trip. Some of it came out on the stairs, under cautions from his father, and very nearly all the rest actually told itself when he met his mother. The story ended with the fact that he had already seen Dr. Harbeck.

"O mother," he said, "he's a real good fellow! Here are the concert tickets!"

"I'm so glad her dress is done!" exclaimed Mrs. Tracy. "She looks so pretty in it!"

"I guess Dr. Harbeck knows what he wants her to go for," said Tom. "Mr. Angus said he understood it."

"I don't, then," began Mr. Tracy.

BEHIND THEM, ON THE SOFA, SAT AMY.

"Husband," interrupted his wife, "you and I must go, too, to take care of Tom and Amy. I'd like some music."

"Of course," said he. "It's business!"

Tom would have given something just then to have shown those tickets to Amy, but she was not thinking of him or of concerts. Late as it was, old Mrs. Cathcart sat by her table, and it was strewn with written papers, and beside her sat Judge Carpenter, reading the mustiest and yellowest of them. Behind them, on the sofa, sat Amy, her sightless eyes closed and a dreamy look upon her face.

"It makes me think so hard, to hear them talk," she said to herself. "I can think a great deal. One face keeps coming and coming, and there's another face close by it."

"Now, Mrs. Cathcart," said the lawyer, "it's time for me to go. As soon as Tom gets back, I shall know what to do. All the people in these houses must pay rent to you, as soon as we can arrange with them."

"Not many of them can pay much rent," she said, "and I don't believe they do."

"All we want is for them to call you the owner, whether they pay or not," said he. "That's putting you in complete possession. It's our point in the law."

"I don't know anything about law," she said, with energy. "It was some lawyers that robbed my husband, and they were robbing Amy's father when he died, and her mother, too, and so Amy and I are poor."

"You and she won't be poor one of these days," said Judge Carpenter; "but it's a good thing you kept on living here, right along, and sticking to it."

He put all the papers into a leather case that he carried, and made just noise enough in walking out to be called a "lubber" by Crib.

Gap Cruden began the next day a little nervously. Jane and Hannah found fault with him because he refused to run out and do some errands for them. Although he was ahead of time in Mr. Gangway's office, the clerks and then Mr. Beckwith came in, looking sour and gloomy. Then Mr. Gangway came in, looking gloomier still, and sat down without a word or nod to Gap.

"I haven't done a thing wrong," Gap was thinking, mournfully, when he suddenly added: "Hello! Here's Tom back again. He's always in luck."

Mr. Gangway's face brightened up, and so did that of Mr. Beckwith. They may have been anxious about Tom, but before Gap could ask him where he had been, the bookkeeper hurried him off on an errand.

"Good-morning, Tom!" said Mr. Gangway, as his hand went out for the sealed envelope Tom delivered to him. "I was just waiting for this. Glad it's come. Did you go out to sea again? Have a good time?"

"Yes, sir, I did," said Tom, "and I've got some other errands to do."

"Go right along and do them," said Mr. Gangway, "and look in here again at the close of the day. I must rush things, myself!"

Not many minutes later, Tom was sitting in an armchair, trying to get over the queer feeling of awe that came to him when he went into the somber, dingy, almost gloomy set of rooms in which Judge Carpenter did his law business.

"The walls are all books," said Tom to himself. "Books on the floor—stacks of papers—"

"Tom," said the lawyer, sharply, looking up from a document he was reading, "now give me his reply."

Tom handed him a pretty thick parcel, and it came open quickly, even nervously.

"Hurrah!" exclaimed Judge Carpenter. "I knew he'd do it! All right! Tom, I was with Mrs. Cathcart last evening. It's all settled. We're going. ahead. I'm glad about Harbeck and the concert. She'll like the music, anyhow. I'll go myself. You come in here to-morrow. We're sure to pin that Cathcart property. Go along, now."

Tom went out, worse puzzled than ever as to what could be the secret of Judge Carpenter's interest and that of Mr. Angus, in a blind girl and an old woman who sold peanuts. He had still two or three errands to do, but it seemed to him that that was about the longest day he had ever known, and it was hot, too. It made him feel hotter, and it tired him to wait and to think about the evening and the concert.

Supper time came, at last, and then there was an hour of excitement and relief, for Tom had to go after Amy. Mrs. Cathcart came with them to the Probus building, to see her granddaughter dressed for the con-

cert, but it was plain that there was some
thing more than that upon her mind. She
had fixed herself a great deal, before leaving
home, while Crib called her all the good and
bad names he knew, and she walked as erect
as a prince all the way to the Probus building, but even after she got there she was
grim and silent.

Miss Higbee and two other ladies had
also arrived, and they had Amy's new white
dress spread out for inspection, and Tom
was sent at once to his own room.

"It's just awful," he exclaimed, when he
shut his door behind him. "I've got to
wear gloves! I can stand it, but I'm glad
there'll be a crowd."

Amy had one advantage that was all her
own. She could hear the women bustling
around and talking, but she could not see
their faces, or the excited manner in which
they pointed, and beckoned, and criticised.

"Pretty as a picture!" remarked Miss
Higbee.

"Beautiful!" said Mrs. Tracy.

"So like her mother!" almost burst from
the shut lips of old Mrs. Cathcart.

Amy could not see the room she stood in,
nor the people in it, but, as she heard that

exclamation, it was just as if she could see, in a kind of dream, a very different room, half full of ladies, dressing with silks, and laces, and flowers, and talking about it all. One of them came and stooped to kiss her, as if she were going away, and just then it was all interrupted by Mrs. Tracy.

"Come in, Tom," she said. "We're all ready. I am so glad I had so much help!"

"Tom Tracy!" exclaimed Miss Higbee. "What a tie! Crooked as it can be!"

There was a large stone in a ring on one of Miss Higbee's fingers, and in the next instant Tom thought she was crowding that bit of shining rock right into his throat. He choked a little, but he endured it, for he was looking admiringly at Amy. He did not try to think much after that. He was a little dazed as to what was going on until he, and his father, and mother, and Amy, were all actually seated in a car of the elevated railway on their way up town.

The opera house was reached in safety, but Tom had failed to make Amy say much on the way. Their tickets provided seats for them in one part of the house, while those obtained by Mr. and Mrs. Tracy were numbered for another locality, and they were separated. It was already pretty nearly full when they went in, and Tom felt more sure that his gloves would not be noticed. A very polite usher took charge of Tom and Amy, and led them away down the middle aisle toward the front. He had become exceedingly polite after one glance at Amy Cathcart's eyes.

"If she can't see I hope she can hear," said the usher to himself, as he led the way, and a score or more of others, ladies and gentlemen, murmured nearly the same thing to each other, as they saw Amy clinging so closely, timidly, to Tom Tracy. All of his own bashfulness had vanished in a courageous feeling that he had somebody depending on him.

"She's blind!" he heard, in a whisper.

"Poor child! See her hand go out."

"How pretty she is! She must love music."

There was something like a stir and a ripple as he and Amy went along. Several seats, secured by Dr. Harbeck, were turned up and waiting, and the usher turned down two for them, and in a moment more the next seat to Amy was turned down.

"Amy," said Tom, "that's Dr. Harbeck."

Amy put out a hand to the doctor, but she could hardly say a word.

"Amy," said the doctor, "this lady next me is Miss Murray. She's very fond of music."

He had more to say, and he said it almost musically, so soft and kind was his voice. So were those of Miss Murray and of a tall gentleman who sat next to her, but Tom knew that they were experts from the great hospital for the blind, and that they were studying Amy's case. It was not deemed well that she should know it that evening.

Tom had never before been in any place that seemed as brilliant as was the opera house. The lights were as yet turned low, so that there was a half dimness, through which came a continual ripple of fluttering fans and suppressed voices. Tom described everything to Amy; the seats, the people, the galleries, the boxes, the drop curtain, and Dr. Harbeck helped him.

The musicians of the orchestra filed into their places, and there was a slight scraping and tuning of fiddles. Tom could feel that Amy was trembling all over at the moment when all the lights flashed suddenly to their brightest blaze. She gave a quick start and made a slight exclamation, and put her hands to her eyes, and Tom saw a brilliant smile on the faces of Dr. Harbeck and his friends. He heard them whisper to each other, and he caught the words, "optic nerve," "temporary paralysis," "suspended sensibility," and some others. Then he heard Miss Murray add: "Beyond all doubt this recovery has been gradual. It is the work of natural forces, and can be perfected by treatment. All I am afraid of is a blunder, a shock. We must say no more, just now."

If a hundred people had been talking around her, Amy Cathcart would not have been aware of it, just then.

She was listening to a long, delicious, wonderful story, told in music by the orchestra. She could not put it into words, but it made her think, think, as she said to herself, and instead of seeing the gay throng in the opera house, she was remembering things that she had forgotten, but which came back to her as they floated upon the stream of that sweet music. The people around her were listening, more or less, but one after another they turned, those of them who could, and looked at the wrapt, silent, happy face of the blind girl. Tom Tracy thought that he had never been so happy in all his life, and he looked at Dr. Harbeck, and was astonished to see how happy his face was and Miss Murray's.

The orchestra finished the story in music, the curtain rose, and a splendidly dressed lady walked out upon the stage that Tom was trying to describe to Amy. He also tried to describe the lady, but he broke down, just as a great storm of applause died away and a hush followed.

"Tom," whispered Amy, "it sounds like a bird!"

"Yes, it does," said Tom, "it's the prima donna," and Amy half arose and leaned forward, listening.

Everybody around them stared at her, and Tom quietly drew her down into her chair, while the exquisite melody of the voice of the prima donna floated through the air, and seemed to Amy to wander all around her, so that she hardly dared to breathe for fear of missing part of it.

"So beautiful, Tom," she said, as the last notes died away and another storm of applause arose from the delighted audience.

CHAPTER XIV.

THE MIDNIGHT FIRE.

THE last notes of the beautiful song died away, and the prima donna seemed to Tom Tracy to have floated off from the stage. He told Amy that loads of bouquets were thrown to her as she disappeared, and there was a great roar of applause while the orchestra helped it with noisy music which Amy said she did not like.

After that the concert went on and there were solos, and duets, and trios, and quartettes of singers, and there were remarkable instrumental performances; and Amy told Tom she was afraid she should not be able to remember any of it.

"Well, no," said Tom, "I guess you won't remember it so that you could play it."

Between the different performances there were a number of short intervals, during which Dr. Harbeck chatted with Amy, as if he had known her all her life, until he got up and went out, and Miss Murray slipped quietly into his place. Tom was particularly glad to have her do so, for it seemed to him as if all the talk had gone out of him, while there was a great plenty of it in Miss Murray.

Right in the middle of the concert there came a pretty long interval, and it hardly surprised Tom at all to see Judge Carpenter get up and leave his own seat, two rods away, and come over for a talk with Amy Cathcart. He talked in a way which made Tom like him better than he ever had before. He, too, went away when the music began again, and not long afterward Miss Murray and the other physician arose and went out, and Tom and Amy were left to themselves. Somehow or other the concert seemed to them to be both long and short, and they could hardly have told which it had been when at last the curtain fell.

"Come, Amy," said Tom, "that's the end of it; it's all over."

"I'm so glad it is," she said, with a very long breath. "I don't want to think any more, I'm so tired. I'm afraid none of the music will ever come back to me, so I can play it."

"I guess it won't," said Tom. "There's too much of it." He helped her with her light wrap, and led her out into the aisle, and he hardly noticed how both ladies and gentlemen made way for them. It seemed to him to be altogether right and natural for people to get out of Amy's way.

Mr. and Mrs. Tracy were waiting for them at the outer door.

"Tom," said his mother, "Dr. Harbeck has sent a carriage to take us home. He says she must not have any more fatigue or excitement to-night, and that you must come and see him to-morrow."

"Now, mother," said Tom, "isn't he just splendid?"

Mrs. Tracy nodded, but she was putting her arm around Amy, as if she were afraid of losing her in the crowd. She kept it there, tightly, until they were all in the carriage and on their way home.

It was a long ride, and it grew wearisome, even with the concert to talk about, but at last they were not a great distance from the Probus building, and Mrs. Tracy said so, as if Amy needed to be encouraged.

"Father," suddenly exclaimed Tom, putting his head out at his side of the carriage, "do you hear that? Look out and see! There's a fire!"

"That's nothing," said Mr. Tracy, quietly. "We're almost home, now. Here we are," he added, as he stepped out upon the sidewalk. "Now, Tom, your mother can go up-stairs. You can take Amy home. I'll stay down at the door to lift the shutters when you get back. I declare, there is a fire!"

"Father," whispered Tom, "it isn't far from her house!"

"Keep still about it," said his father, in a low voice. "She mustn't—"

"Don't tell her," began Mrs. Tracy, but it was too late. Amy must have heard something, for she sprang to her feet, exclaiming: "Grandmother! Tom! Tom! I want to get home!"

"Tom," said his mother, "the sooner she gets there the better. Now, Amy, nothing is the matter. Everything is all right. Tom's going to take you right, straight home—"

"But the fire!" exclaimed Amy.

"That's nothing," said Mr. Tracy, positively. "There are fires all the while. Don't you be worried about it."

And then he said to Thomas, in an under-tone that was full of reproof: "Thomas, you ought not to have said anything about it, so she could hear you. A boy that speaks too quick isn't worth a cent."

The cluster of old-time buildings, some of brick and some of wood, on the corner of Garnet and Burgoyne streets, was shabby enough, and rickety enough to entirely justify the people who spoke of it as "an old rookery." It looked as if the patched, irregular structures leaned against each other as if they needed to be held up. When-ever anybody asked who owned that prop-erty he was likely to be told "it's in law." That meant that the title to it had been so long in dispute that it was hidden away among law-suits and cross-suits, and could not easily be found. So the old buildings had nobody to keep them in repair, and they were rotting and crumbling away. They were a sort of eye-sore, and they were a great hindrance to the growth and improve-ment of that neighborhood.

Mrs. Cathcart had not remained at the Probus building that evening for a great while after Amy and the others went away to the concert. Neither had Miss Higbee

16

and her friends. All that part of the city, in fact, looked very much as if everybody had gone home at the hour when the cry of "Fire! Fire! Fire!" ran out along the deserted streets.

In the daytime there would have been at once a rush and a gathering crowd, but now there was very little material left to make a crowd out of, and the cry did not find many voices to take it up and make it echo back and forth among the tall, silent buildings.

In a few minutes more, a steam fire engine came dashing along, its big, splendid horses galloping furiously, and the smoke pouring in black puffs from its brazen chimney. At a little distance behind it rattled a hose-cart, and upon both machines were firemen clinging like so many human bees in uniform. Clatter, clang, rattle, dash, another and another engine came madly plunging along the streets, but as yet the only indication Tom could get at the Probus building of the precise place of that fire were the shouts, the directions taken by the engines, and a cloud of smoke with a faint light of fire that was thrown upon that cloud.

"I guess it must be pretty nigh," remarked old Mrs. Cathcart, as she sat at her window, waiting for Amy to come home. "They put out fires mighty quick, nowadays, compared to how they let 'em burn when I was a girl. I do wish that child would come. She'll be all tired to death. I don't know about letting her go out in this way. That there doctor! Well, I'm afraid it's of no use!"

Several minutes went by, and all the while the noise and confusion rapidly increased. Then it seemed to come sweeping around the corner into Garnet street, and Mrs. Cathcart leaned out to look and listen.

"Is it as near as that?" she exclaimed.

Bang, bang, bang, at that moment thundered the club of a policeman on the door of her room, at the head of the stairs, while he shouted: "Up! Get up! Get out! Open the door! Fire! Everybody get out of this building!"

She drew in her head and hurried to open the door.

"Pack up fast, madame," he said. "Nothing on earth can stop that fire. These old shells of buildings are a perfect tinder-box."

"Oh, dear!" she exclaimed. "Amy! Amy!" and then she said to the policeman: "The

fire! Is it in the stables or is it in the paint
shop? Where is it?"

"Paint, oil, kerosene, hay," he said. "It
burns like a match factory. Boys!" he
shouted down the stairs, "come on! Help
the old woman out!"

At that very instant a carriage came
rattling down Burgoyne street, and it was
halted by the police in full view of the puff-
ing steam fire engines and the increasing
blaze.

"You can't get any nearer," said an
officer.

"Why, we've got to get there," said Tom,
as he sprang out. "That's where she
lives."

"I'll stay here," shouted the driver of the
carriage. "You can bring any of her folks
right here."

"Grandmother!" screamed Amy. "She's
there alone! Tom!"

"Be still, Amy," said Tom. "Don't you
be frightened. She won't be hurt."

"Go right along and get her," said the
cool policeman. "It's right good luck for
her that you've got a carriage. The young
lady mustn't go."

"She's blind," gasped Tom. "Her grandmother lives in one of those houses that are burning."

"Blind!" cried the officer. "Well, we'll answer for her safety, but she must stay where she is. Go and fetch the old woman. Quick, now! It's all going like a flash. Jump!"

"Amy," said Tom, "I must go and do all I can. You stay here."

He was in more than a little doubt as to whether he ought not to stay and take care of her; but she decided for him.

"Grandmother! Grandmother!" she said. "She'll get burned! Go, Tom! Quick!"

Off he darted, and the next words she uttered were heard only by the driver and the officer, but both of them tried hard to make her feel sure that nobody was in any danger of being burned up.

Poor Amy! Her beautiful evening of music and song was ending mournfully. Here she was, all alone in a carriage, in the street, at nearly midnight, while her home was burning down.

There was a tremendous amount of noise being made, and the fire was brightening fiercely at the moment when Tom sprang up the stairway and into the room.

"Mrs. Cathcart!" he shouted.

"Amy, where is she?" she screamed in reply. "She ain't here, is she?"

"She's in the carriage," said Tom, "and I've come after you. We can take a lot of the trunks in it, too."

He hardly knew what she said next, for he went to work at once. The policeman and two other men had already accomplished something, catching up and carrying down stairs boxes and furniture and trunks and anything they could pick up.

"There!" Tom heard her say, as one trunk went out, "that one's got all the papers in it. I'm glad that's safe."

"Out! Out!" shouted the officer. "Here it comes! Kerosene! Faugh!" ·

The back windows were open, and at that moment a strong puff of wind came through them, bringing with it a volume of smoke, quickly followed by angry tongues of fire. That part of the rookery had just kindled, but it would surely burn like the rest. Tom had been snatching up everything he could see that belonged particularly to Amy, and he now made a loaded journey to the street, while Mrs. Cathcart came down behind the men who were carrying her last lot of trunks.

"The piano 'll have to go," said Tom, regretfully, as he sprang up stairs again.

"Come back!" shouted the nearest officer. "You mustn't try it again. You'll be stifled!"

He was too late with his warning for Tom was already half way up, and in a moment more he was in the room. He had thought of one small trunk in the bed-room, full of things belonging to Amy, and he had determined to rescue it. Twice he was forced back from the door of that room by strong puffs of smoke, but he was not to be driven entirely from his purpose.

"I've got it!" he shouted at his third rush. "Oh, my eyes! Phew!"

"Mew! Mew! Me-ew-ew!" sounded at his feet.

"Come along, Whitey," he said, as he picked her up. "Now I'll try and get out Pete and Crib."

The parrot had been in a state of wild excitement from the moment when his slumbers had been disturbed by the bang of the policeman's club upon the door. He was sitting then upon his swinging perch over the geraniums, and he began at once trying to imitate the cries he heard. He did pretty well with "Out," but not quite so well with "fire." As the racket went on, he hooked himself down among the geraniums, and from under their cover he hurled out all the hard words he knew in more languages than one, including his own, native, parrot language.

Pete was quite as excited as was Crib, and he was singing as if for dear life when Tom reached up for his cage. He sent out a long, piercing trill as he felt himself lifted and then lowered, and he was answered by an unearthly screech from Crib.

"Crib," said Tom, "I'm afraid I can't carry you this trip."

"Luff! Luff! You lubber!" screeched Crib, fiercely, with a frightened spread of wings and an out-reaching beak. "Port! Peanuts! Great Crib!"

"I'm loaded! Oh, that smoke!" said Tom, as he swung the little trunk on one shoulder, gathered the kitten into his bosom, and picked up the canary.

The smoke was, indeed, blowing in furiously through the back windows as Tom

made his way to the door. Down he went
into the street, to find Mrs. Cathcart trying
to break away from an officer and come
after him.

"OH, THAT SMOKE!"

"Tom!" she exclaimed, "oh, I'm so glad
you got out! I was afraid we'd lost you.

Dear me! Amy's trunk, and Pete, and the kitten!"

"They're all right," said Tom. "Now I'm going to save old Crib."

"You're not going up those stairs again," said the officer, quietly, but firmly. "Do you hear that?"

Tom stood still and listened. In a moment he understood what the policeman meant, and it made him shudder all over. What he heard was the roaring, crackling, threatening sound of hot flames driven by a rising wind through the dry lumber of that rookery. Nothing could stand before such a fire-blast as that. The firemen had shown good judgment in directing all their efforts to the rescue of persons and the saving of loose property. Almost everybody who lived there had been sound asleep when the fire broke out. After they were taken care of, about all that could be hoped for was to keep the fire from spreading to other and more valuable buildings near by or adjoining.

"It's just a furnace!" said one fireman.

"It was about time all those old concerns were either burned up or pulled down," remarked another.

"Poor Crib!" exclaimed Mrs. Cathcart. "And the piano! And all the rest of the furniture! And it isn't insured! It's all got to go!"

"I did just want to save him," said Tom, "but I couldn't."

"Great Crib!" came a frantic scream through the open window, and at that moment there was a large explosion, a great, red flash, a crash, and a still blacker volume of smoke. That was followed by an increased roaring of wind, and the fire poured out of the windows.

"Poor Crib's gone!" said Mrs. Cathcart. "Oh, I'm so glad you didn't go up stairs again!"

"It'd ha' been the last of him if he'd ha' tried it on," said the officer who had held Tom back.

"Come, Mrs. Cathcart," said Tom. "We must get away. You and Amy are to come to our house."

"It's the best thing in the world she wasn't here," exclaimed her grandmother, excitedly. "Hurry! I want to see her right away! She'll be scared to death!"

CHAPTER XV.

THE NEW DAY.

THE fire had been as great a disaster to scores of other people as it had to the Cathcarts, and perhaps greater, but they had all been helped as well as was possible. The streets were littered in all directions with the things which had been snatched up and carried out, and Tom caught himself wondering whether anybody would ever be able to say whose anything might be in such a higgledy-piggledy mix as that.

When he and Mrs. Cathcart came away from Garnet street, she was carrying a heavy valise in one hand, but she was too much excited, and so was Tom, to notice that she was lugging along in the other a great basket of peanuts, oranges, and candy. He had stuck to the little trunk and the bird cage, but Pete was entirely silent, now, while Whitey, in her fright, was digging her sharp little claws clean through Tom's new

clothes and into him, and was mewing piti-
fully.

Away around on Burgoyne street, at the
outer edge of the confusion, stood Dr. Harbeck's carriage, and back in a corner of it,
with her face against the side, cowered poor
Amy. Her eyes were tightly closed and she
was trembling from head to foot. It was
all so strange and terrible to a girl who had
lived so long in one place, of only two rooms,
and all in the dark. It seemed to her that
there was nothing but noise, noise, noise,
and she could not understand it at all. Suddenly there came in among the other sounds
one that was very pleasant to hear.

"Here we are, Amy!" shouted Tom, as he
came hurrying to the carriage.

"O Amy!" exclaimed Mrs. Cathcart, at
the same moment, but she could not say
another word.

"Amy," added Tom, "we're all right.
I've got Pete here, and Whitey, but Crib's
burned up! Poor fellow!"

"Poor fellow! Poor Crib! Oh, I'm so
sorry! Oh, I'm so glad you've come!" said
the blind girl, and, as she reached out her
hands, Tom put the mewing, frightened kitten into them.

She had something to take care of now, and it seemed to do her good, for she was very quiet while they loaded the carriage with trunks and other things. Then Mrs. Cathcart climbed in and put her arms around her granddaughter, but then, she, too, sat still, as if she were in a kind of dream, and did not know what to make of it.

"Probus building," shouted Tom to the driver, as he sprang in, but it was not until just before they got there that Amy lifted her head from Mrs. Cathcart's shoulder and said to him: "Tom, I saw the fire!"

"Did you?" exclaimed Tom. "I must see Dr. Harbeck! Father! Mother! I must go and see him, and I must go and tell Judge Carpenter, right away."

Mrs. Tracy had refused to go up to her rooms, and so both of them were there, waiting, and they were eager to take possession of Amy and her grandmother.

"We'll take the best kind of care of you, ma'am," said Mr. Tracy.

' Dear child!" exclaimed Mrs. Tracy. "You must be scared to death."

"I'm so glad I'm here!" said Amy, hugging her.

"TOM," SHE SAID, "WHEN I WAS BLIND, I USED TO THINK AND DREAM ABOUT SEEING."—Page 269.

"Go ahead, Tom!" shouted Mr. Tracy. "Don't forget anything you ought to 'tend to."

"Dr. Harbeck's, first," said Tom to the driver, as the carriage started.

It seemed to him a long drive before he could pull the doctor's night-bell and bring him down to the door to hear a report of what had happened at the fire. Dr. Harbeck asked only a few questions, and at the end of them he said: "Keep her in a dark room. I will be there in the morning. There must not be one ray of light. Put a bandage over her eyes until I see her."

He closed the door, and Tom was relieved of his first, great errand, but the carriage was gone now, and he was on foot. He had not a great distance to walk, however, before a pull at another bell brought out Judge Carpenter to hear what had occurred at Garnet and Burgoyne streets. The lawyer seemed a great deal more excited than the doctor had been.

"Best thing that could have happened!" he exclaimed. "I'll be dressed in no time You wait for me. We must stir up the contractors."

17

Tom could only guess what was meant by that, but in a few minutes he and the judge were out in the streets together.

"There are just three men for me to see," said the judge.

Three houses were visited, therefore, of men whose business it was to manage other men in starting work upon big buildings, and then he and Tom hurried away down town.

"I want to see just how clean a job the fire has made to begin with," said the lawyer. "If it burned as well as you say it did, there's a great difficulty burned out of our way."

They were almost at the corner of Garnet and Burgoyne streets when Tom exclaimed: "Why, it's daylight!" and in a moment more he added: "Yes, sir, pretty much everything was burned up."

"Thorough work!" said the lawyer. "About as complete and clean a burn up as I ever saw. Hello! If here isn't McCarthy with a gang of his men!"

It was a fact! Thanks to the promptness of Tom Tracy, the first gang of the men who worked for Mr. Angus' contractors were in possession of the ruins at daylight of the morning after the fire. Gang after gang joined them, so that when business men came down town they found at least a hundred laborers there, with teams and drivers, clearing the ground upon which, they were told, Mr. Angus was about to erect a splendid, ten-story, fire-proof building, to be called the Cathcart building, after the name of the old New York family from whom he had bought the land it was to stand upon.

Amy Cathcart's eyes were the only pair in the Probus building that closed during that night of excitement.

The room she was first placed in was lighted but dimly, and she was not left alone. Mrs. Tracy refused to lie down until Tom's return, and her husband seemed disposed to walk up and down, and to be listening all the while for the door-bell.

Tom's prolonged absence made matters worse instead of better, and when he did come, with his other news and Dr. Harbeck's orders, he created quite a sensation.

"Do just as the doctor says," said Mr. Tracy, sternly. "She might open her eyes! Bandage them!"

Then there came a general hush, as if sounds might be dangerous as well as light.

As soon as Amy was cared for, according to the prescription, Mrs. Tracy went into the kitchen to arrange for an early breakfast, while her husband went out, as he said, "for a good look at those ruins," and Tom was ordered to lie down.

He was made to go to his own room and lie down again after he had eaten his breakfast, but he did not know that he had been asleep at all when his father shook him wide awake and said, "Tom!"

"Father," said Tom, opening his eyes, "has Dr. Harbeck come to see Amy?"

"He has come and gone," said Mr. Tracy. "Judge Carpenter's been here, too, and if a telegram doesn't get here by noon from Mr. Angus, he and Mr. Gangway want you to do another long errand. It's about noon now. Get up. A boy that can't stand being awake a night or so isn't worth a cent."

Tom sprang to his feet, exclaiming, "All right, father. I'm ready."

There was no one to tell him about Dr. Harbeck's visit to Amy. Miss Murray had come with him, and Mrs. Tracy said they "were such quiet, unconcerned sort of people."

They chatted with Amy about the concert, and her own music, and the lost piano, and poor Crib, and she grew more and more composed as they went along.

"Miss Murray," she asked, at length, "was it the smoke in my eyes that made them prick so when it puffed out of the window with the fire?"

"Did you rub your eyes?" asked Miss Murray.

"No, I didn't," said Amy. "But it hurt them to look at the fire, and I shut them. How bright it was!"

The doctor nodded, and Miss Murray nodded, and pretty soon afterward they arose and went out into the other room.

"Is there—is there any hope for her?" eagerly asked Mrs. Tracy.

"Not the least," said Dr. Harbeck, "unless she is kept from using her eyes until this shock has passed away."

"We'll see to that," exclaimed Mrs. Tracy. "You can depend on us!"

"I believe we can," said Miss Murray, and she and the doctor went away.

"They are angels, Mrs. Tracy," said Mrs. Cathcart. "And I do believe you're another, and Tom's another."

Tom did not feel one bit like an angel when he came out to eat his dinner, and to receive a message calling him to meet Judge Carpenter at Rufus Gangway's office.

"I've got to go somewhere again, I suppose," he said to his father.

"Go ahead," said Mr. Tracy. "A boy that can't do an errand isn't worth a cent."

He was not even permitted to speak to Amy before going, and he went off in great discontent, taking his alligator-leather grip-sack with him, all packed, leaving his mother almost angry because she did not know where her son was to be sent.

"He's off to China again," muttered Gap Cruden to himself when he saw Tom Tracy sitting by Judge Carpenter and Mr. Gangway, and then he saw him go away without saying one word to anybody else.

Four days after that, a very beautiful schooner yacht, with all sails set, came drifting before a light wind into the harbor of Portland, in the state of Maine. Against a post on one of the piers of the harbor leaned an anxious, tired-out looking boy, at whose feet lay a plump bag of alligator-leather. "The Rover!" he shouted, snatching up his bag. "She's got here!"

Not many minutes later a couple of gentlemen on the deck of the yacht had their attentions called to a rowboat that was pulling toward her.

"Hurrah, Captain Andrews!" said one of them. "Here comes Tom!"

"That's so," said the captain, laughing. "I guess you'll have to keep that boy."

"Keep him? Of course I will," said Mr. Angus. "He's just the boy I want."

On board came Tom, but not until he was in the cabin did he tell how long he had waited in Portland.

"We'll take the next train for New York," was the most important remark made by Mr. Angus after hearing about the fire and reading his letters. "Sorry for the parrot, but we'll buy her a new piano."

The Rover reached a wharf, and then Mr. Angus and Tom reached a railway train, and then there was a swift, tiresome, day-and-night journey. Tom was beginning to understand the Cathcart business pretty well, but he knew better than to ask Mr. Angus any questions about it. He discovered on the way, however, that the money king could talk right along about anything in the world excepting business.

"Tom," said he, at last, when they were within half an hour's ride of the great city, "if you only knew enough, I'd take you right into my office."

"Knew enough?" echoed Tom, with a great gulp of disappointment swelling in his throat.

"That's it," said the money king. "You know some things pretty well to begin with, but there's too much that you don't know. I want you to spend a year in a business college, learning all they teach there, and then a year in a banker's and merchant's office. You must learn French, and Spanish, and German, and English—"

"English?" said Tom. "I know that."

"No, you don't," said Mr. Angus. "You must learn to write and speak it better than you do now. Arithmetic, geography—"

"I got them at school," said Tom. "I got a hundred in geography."

"A good beginning," said Mr. Angus. "I don't know as much arithmetic as I ought to, and geography is one of my weak spots.

There are whole counties, and railways, and rivers, and mountain ranges in this country, and all over the world, that I know very little about. I get stuck every now and then."

"I can't afford it," began Tom, but he was interrupted.

"Do you remember the ten dollars you wouldn't take?" asked Mr. Angus. "Well, the interest on that, the way I'll fix it, and what you've earned by these errands, 'll pay your way. As soon as you know enough, I've a place for you."

Tom found it hard to say anything, and Mr. Angus had no more to say until after they reached the city.

"It's early in the day, Tom," he remarked. "You go home and see your folks and then come to Mr. Gangway's. Tell Amy I've been appointed her guardian. Tell her I hope she'll see the new Cathcart building some day."

"I hope she will," said Tom, excitedly. "But mother and I'll take care of her if she never sees anything."

"Good for you, Tom," said the money king, and they separated. But Tom went down town with a strong feeling that he

wanted to see Amy's property before even
going to the Probus building. A great sur-
prise was ready for him at the corner of
Garnet and Burgoyne streets. It was a
great hole in the ground, going down deeper
at a rapid rate, to receive the foundations of
a tall building. Tom stared at it for a few
minutes and turned away, and he hardly
seemed to himself to know what had happened there until after he had been some
time in the ninth story of the Probus building, talking with his mother and Mrs. Cathcart and Amy. He had some business to
attend to for Mr. Angus that day and on
other days which followed, but there was a
great deal of time almost every day when
he could sit and talk to Amy in her dark
room. Mr. Angus himself came several
times, and Tom liked him better after hearing his hard, rasping, business voice grow
soft and soothing when he talked to the
blind girl. Dr. Harbeck came also again
and again, and at the end of a fortnight
Miss Murray spent a night in the Probus
building. She slept with Amy, but she arose
toward morning while it was yet dark, and
quietly called in the rest of them, one by
one. Amy awoke, and she heard them talk-

ing around her, but it did not seem to startle her. The room was very dark, and Tom knew that the bandage had been removed from Amy's eyes while she was asleep, and that the result would be declared as the day dawned. His heart beat fast then, but that was nothing to the way it fluttered when the blackness of that room at last began to melt, so that he could see the doorway.

"Amy, darling," said Miss Murray, softly, "do not close your eyelids. Keep them open."

The light grew rapidly, but gradually, until Tom could see that Amy was sitting up and was pressing both hands upon her heart. A little brighter came the promise of the sunrise glory, and Amy looked wistfully around her.

"Grandmother?" she whispered. "Yes, it is grandmother. Miss Murray? Dear Miss Murray! Tom's mother? Tom? O Tom! O mother! I can see you all!"

"Mother? I guess it is mother!" exclaimed Mrs. Tracy, hugging Amy hard. "Tom's mother! Your mother! I've always wanted a daughter! My little girl!"

Old Mrs. Cathcart was kneeling by the bed, just then, shaking all over, but she did not utter a word for more than a minute. Miss Murray's face was beautiful, Tom thought. She made Mrs. Tracy let go of Amy, so she could put on a kind of green shade above her eyes and make her drink something from a tumbler.

"You must have another nap," she said.

"I want to see how Tom looks, first," said Amy. "O Tom! I can see!"

"Amy," blurted out Tom, "you go to sleep. You're going to learn how to see as well as I can."

A little later in the day, Tom stood before Dr. Harbeek, holding out a handful of greenbacks.

"Keep them, Tom," said the doctor, "I'm paid for Amy's case, but I'm glad you followed my prescription about that money."

A few days afterward Mr. Angus came and carried Amy away, but for all that, Tom Tracy lost the rest of his summer vacation. He had to spend it in taking Mrs. Cathcart and Amy around, everywhere, to show Amy things she had never before seen.

Gap Cruden remarked about it that he "guessed Tom Tracy's in Chiny pretty much all the while," but then Gap found himself in a very good place at Mr. Gangway's, and he was beginning to feel fairly sure of keeping it.

*   *   *   *   *   *

Seven days make a week, and seven years make a week of years. So it was just a little more than a week of years, after all that, when a very pretty young lady stood on the deck of a steamship that was steaming out of New York harbor. She wore a new, gold ring upon one of her fingers, and beside her stood a tall young man.

"Tom," she said, "isn't the city beautiful! I'm almost sorry to leave it. Everything is beautiful now. Everything used to seem to me like a kind of dark prison."

"Well, Amy, so it was," he said, "but there's light enough now. I want you to see all of the world you can,—other cities; everything worth seeing—before we get back from Europe."

"Tom," she said, "when I was blind, I used to think and dream about seeing. How wonderful it all is!"

And so Tom and Amy sailed away.